L. FRANK BAUM

THE WONDERFUL WIZARD OF OZ

THE ONLY AUTHORIZED EDITION

THE WONDERFUL WIZARD OF OZ

THE AUTHORIZED
100th ANNIVERSARY EDITION

L. FRANK BAUM

New Illustrations by
WILLIAM STOUT

Original Illustrations by
W. W. DENSLOW

ibooks
new york
www.ibooksinc.com

DISTRIBUTED BY SIMON & SCHUSTER

For
Blaire Preiss

William Stout's "Wicked Witch of the East" appears far more sinister than her sister from the West.

TABLE OF CONTENTS

This William Stout "Tin Man" was inspired by his affection for the John R. Neill *Oz* illustrations.

INTRODUCTION
by Robert A. Baum

"I am Oz, the Great and Terrible. Who are you, and why do you seek me?" These words were written one hundred years ago and readers are still seeking Oz today. Hardly a day passes without our hearing a "Hi, Munchkin," "Toto, I don't think we're in Kansas anymore," "Follow the Yellow Brick Road," or the classic "There's no place like home." Oz has become a part of our everyday life the world over.

I have often wondered what went through L. Frank Baum's mind as he held the first copy of his new book, of *The Wonderful Wizard of Oz*? Did he have any idea of the effect it would have one hundred years later? I feel that it is very fitting that Oz is having its one hundredth anniversary on the start of the new millennium. The fact that we are still celebrating Oz proves that Oz transcends across all time and events. The success of the book, and the stories people still tell about their first encounters with Oz, lead me to believe that my L. Frank Baum was truly a Wizard. As his great-grandson, I only wish that he were alive today to see how Oz has become a part of people's everyday lives, no matter what part of the world they live in.

With these thoughts in mind, I would like to share my first memory of *The Wonderful Wizard of Oz* with you. It happened when I was almost seven years old. You must remember this was before the days of television. It was 1949, and the MGM movie was being re-released. I went with my parents and grandparents to a local theatre to see the film for the first time. There was an air of excitement as we took our seats in the front row. I can vividly remember craning my neck to see the opening credits as they appeared at the beginning of the film. Suddenly, at the bottom of the screen in big letters I saw, FROM THE BOOK BY L. FRANK BAUM. Just at that moment, my father leaned over and whispered to me, "That's your great-grandfather!" I had known that for a while, but to see his name so big, and ON A MOVIE SCREEN . . . wow! The power of Oz began to magically enter my life.

Until my father whispered those unforgettable words in my ear, Oz had never taken on a major role in the family. We did, however, share stories about L. Frank at family gatherings and holiday dinners. Of course, everyone was proud of L. Frank's success, but other than that, it was not a big subject of discussion. However, those unforgettable words my father whispered in my ear changed everything.

From that moment in the movie theatre until now, Oz

has continued to work its magic on my life. Not only did the family stories about L. Frank Baum take on a new and deeper meaning for me, they also began to give me a better understanding of why *Oz* has become so popular and continues to work its way into our daily lives. Please allow me to share with you some of my experiences and insights I have found on my journey down the "Yellow Brick Road."

My first memorable experience came a number of years later, while enrolled in a boarding school. It was the custom for the professors and their families to each head a table in the dining hall. The students would change tables every three weeks so that we would become acquainted with the professors. The wife of my English professor shared with me her passion for Oz. In the early 1920s, as she boarded a train for college, her parents gave her twenty dollars. She knew they had saved a long time for the money, and that it was to last for the entire semester. With an hour layover at one station, she went for a walk around the town. In a store window she saw a set of fourteen *Oz* books. She eyed them for a while as she considered her money. When the train pulled out of the station, she had fourteen *Oz* books and only two dollars and fifty cents left for college!

What impressed me the most was the fact that she was willing to go without so that she could be the proud owner of a set of *Oz* books. She told me that the *Oz* characters had become her friends, and had given her a connection to home each time she read the stories. She kept the books in her family, read them to her children, and then her grandchildren. Oz had become a part of her family tradition, too.

I have developed a deeper understanding and apprecia-
tion for my great-grandfather's work throughout my pro-
fessional career as a teacher. My wife, Clare, and I had
already taught elementary school for fifteen years when we
decided to try reading *The Wonderful Wizard of Oz* in our
classrooms. We wanted a book that would both excite and
educate our students. We felt *Oz* would do both. We were
even able to convince the principal to allow the departure
from "recommended" books.

The students and I would read the book and compare it
to the MGM movie. Clare used the stories and characters in
the book and movie to discuss goal setting and teamwork.
The students then created an original *Oz* poster and story,
with their favorite character, to emphasize a moral or idea.
Year after year, the power of Oz continued to capture the
imagination and interest of our students.

The powerful effect of Oz even carried over to the drama
teacher. In one production of *The Wizard of Oz*, the part of
the Cowardly Lion was played by a seemingly shy student.
Once the costume went on, he became the Cowardly Lion,
animated and roaring. Returning to school years later, he
took the time to look us up and let us know he had truly
gotten a Badge of Courage from the Great Oz.

While Clare and I were on sabbatical in 1989, I was con-
tacted by Dreamer Productions. They were about to begin
filming *Dreamer of Oz*, a movie about L. Frank Baum's life
leading up to *The Wonderful Wizard of Oz*. The movie was
to star John Ritter as L. Frank and Annette O'Toole as his
wife, Maud. The director, Jack Bender, could not find anyone who would let their *Oz* collection be borrowed for the

production. After I had spoken with him I realized that the power of Oz yet again changed my life. I knew my collection, much of it from L. Frank, would add to the authenticity of the film. It was as if I had been given the collection just for this film.

The production company easily solved the problem of handling the books by making me part of the cast and crew. My job would be to set up all the scenes needing Baum books. As an added bonus, Clare and my two daughters, Christine and Carolyn, were given parts in the film. A number of events took place during filming that gave me great insight as to the power of Oz. They also helped me understand what my great-grandfather must have gone through in writing and publishing *The Wonderful Wizard of Oz*.

The first event came as Clare and I met John Ritter for the first time. As he stepped from his trailer and we were introduced, we could not say a word. It was not John Ritter who had stepped out, but my great-grandfather. We could only point to the picture of L. Frank that I had brought. The resemblance was uncanny.

The second occurrence came in a scene, late at night, in which L. Frank is venting his frustration at not finding a publisher for *The Wonderful Wizard of Oz*. Sitting at his desk, he picks up three pencils and slowly breaks each one on his chest. John Ritter did the scene with such feeling, that it was difficult to watch. Later I spoke to John and told him how the scene had impacted me. He said, "I know the pain your great-grandfather was going through. It hurts."

The most powerful display came in a quiet moment when John Ritter shared with Annette O'Toole the inscription L. Frank had written to Maud in a copy of *Mother Goose in Prose*. As they sat in a swing on the set, a wardrobe person snapped a Polaroid picture. When it came out, there was a bright halo around the entire picture.

Perhaps the best part for me was working with the crew. As I got to know many of them, I was impressed by their dedication and commitment to their craft. They came early and left late, doing whatever was necessary to get it done right. The extra effort came from their love of Oz. They took special pride in being part of something Oz. I have found this phenomenon to be a common occurrence.

I treasure all of the experiences they shared with me as they again helped remind me of why Oz has become so universal. The entire experience was like stepping back into my great-grandfather's time.

My most recent discovery was when my wife and I traveled to Chittenango, New York, the birthplace of my great-grandfather. We were invited to be the Grand Marshals for their annual Ozfest and parade that occur each June. We arrived several days early so we could explore the surrounding area and all of the places L. Frank Baum had lived and worked. Few of the actual buildings are still standing, but with some imagination we could get a sense of what life as a child must have been like in his day.

Standing at these places, it was easy to see that life on the farm and surrounding countryside must have had a tremendous impact on a growing child's mind. Frank and his siblings were free to roam the estate or wander in the woods while their imagination took flight. Frank did not have much of a formal education and I credit this fact for much of his success. I am positive it allowed his childhood imagination to remain intact throughout his life. Even though his parents were considered "doting," he grew up being able to experiment, fail, and learn from his mistakes. I feel it is this combination of childhood experiences that set the stage for his future writing, especially *The Wonderful Wizard of Oz*.

The most important discovery came as my wife and I stood in the very parlor where his sister, Harriet Neal Baum, introduced Frank to Maud Gage. It brought to mind the same scene from *Dreamer of Oz*. In this scene, Harriet tells Frank that "she was sure he would just love her" (Maud), and I could imagine Frank standing there in front of her and saying, "Consider yourself loved, Miss Gage."

Thinking back on this scene from *Dreamer of Oz*, and standing in the very parlor where my great-grandparents met, I now had a complete picture. I understood what they saw in each other. It was truly love at first sight. In that instant, Maud saw the potential in my great-grandfather. She devoted the rest of her life to making sure that his imagination had free reign to blossom. He saw the woman of his dreams. The woman who brought out the best in him. Someone he could share his dreams with. Together they walked down the "Yellow Brick Road."

Often the most complex of questions has the simplest of answer; such is the case with *Oz*. All of my experiences lead me to but one conclusion, and the reason for his success is plain: he never lost sight of the audience he wrote for. He wrote to entertain children of all ages, while looking at the world through the eyes of a child, just one step beyond reality. Oz is a home away from home, where dreams are real and reality can be put aside. Oz is imagination unleashed, allowing all who enter to soar somewhere over the rainbow.

Thank you for allowing me to share some of my adventures and experiences in Oz with you. I hope, as you read this volume, whether for the first time or the hundredth, that it brings you and your family as much joy as it has brought mine.

Ozily yours,

Robert A. Baum

2000

The Wonderful World of Oz Presents

Essays

In this William Stout design for the "Oz Aerial Adventures" ride within the *Wonderful Wizard of Oz*-themed Entertainment Resort, airships await travelers in the Pre-Boarding Area as guests wait to be transported on an aerial tour of Oz.

Previous page: Sample cover sheet for the scripts written for the various proposed ride attractions for the *Wonderful Wizard of Oz*-themed Entertainment Resort. Art by William Stout.

OZ IS US

Celebrating the Wizard's centennial

by John Updike

A hundred years ago, *The Wonderful Wizard of Oz*, by L. Frank Baum, was published by the soon-to-be-defunct Chicago-based firm of George M. Hill. The Library of Congress is hosting a commemorative exhibition, and Norton has brought out a centennial edition of *The Annotated Wizard of Oz*, edited and annotated by Michael Patrick Hearn ($39.95). Hearn, we learn from a preface by Martin Gardner, became a Baum expert while he was an English major at Bard College, and put forward an annotated *Wizard* when he was only twenty years old. Gardner, the polymathic compiler of *The Annotated Alice* (1960) and *More Annotated Alice* (1960), had been invited to do the same, in 1970, for Baum's fable; disclaiming competence, he recommended the young Bard Baumist to Clarkson N. Potter, who published Hearn's tome in 1973. In the years since, Hearn has produced annotated versions of Charles Dickens's *Christmas Carol* and Mark Twain's *Huckleberry Finn*, added to the vast tracts of Baum scholarship, co-authored a biography of W. W. Denslow, the *Wizard*'s illustrator, and labored at a still unpublished "definitive biography" of Baum. Presumably, he and Norton have been patiently waiting, with fresh slews of annotation and illustration, for the centennial (which is also that of Dreiser's *Sister Carrie*, Conrad's *Lord Jim*, Colette's first Claudine novel, and Freud's *Interpretation of Dreams*) to roll around.

It is not hard to imagine why Gardner ducked the original assignment. The two *Alice* books are more literate, intricate, and modernist than Baum's *Wonderful Wizard*, and Lewis Carroll's mind, laden with mathematical lore, chess moves, semantic puzzles, and the riddles of Victorian religion, was more susceptible to explication, at least by the like-minded Gardner. But Baum, Hearn shows in his introduction, was a complicated character, too—a Theosophist, an expert on poultry, a stagestruck actor and singer, a fine amateur photographer, an inventive household tinkerer, a travelling china salesman, and only by a final shift, a children's writer. He was forty-four when *The Wonderful Wizard of Oz* was published. His prior bibliography included a directory of stamp dealers, a treatise on the mating and management of Hamburg chickens, a definitive work entitled *The Art of Decorating Dry Goods Windows and Interiors* (also celebrating its centennial), and a few small volumes for children. Baum's life (1856–1919) reflects the economic and ideological adventurism of his America. Hearn tells us that his father, Benjamin Ward Baum, "followed nearly as many careers as his son would. He was building a barrel factory in Chittenango [New York] when the boy was born, but made a fortune in the infant Pennsylvania oil industry only a few years later." Lyman Frank, one of nine children, of whom five survived into adulthood, was raised on a luxurious estate in Syracuse and educated by English tutors. He was a dreamy reader of a boy. He lasted only two years at Peekskill Military School, and went on to Syracuse Classical School, without, apparently, graduating. He married the twenty-year-old Maud Gage when he was twenty-six and, grown into a lanky man with a large mustache, was touring as the star of a musical melodrama, *The Maid of Arran*, which he had written—book, lyrics, and music. His mother-in-law, Matilda Joslyn Gage, was a prominent feminist and a keen Theosophist; she had not wanted her daughter to leave Cornell to marry an actor. But Maud did anyway, and when she became pregnant Frank left the theatre. With his uncle, Adam Baum, he established Baum's Castorine Company, marketing an axle grease invented by his brother Benjamin and still, in this slippery world, being manufactured.

Maud's sisters and brother had all settled in the Dakota Territory; in 1888 Frank moved with his family to Aberdeen, South Dakota, where he opened a variety store, Baum's Bazaar. Drought and depression caused the store to fail; in 1890 Baum took over a weekly newspaper, calling it the *Saturday Pioneer*, and by 1891 it, too, was failing. He found employment in Chicago, first as a reporter and then as a travelling salesman with the wholesale china-and-glassware firm of Pitkin & Brooks. The two-and-a-half-year Dakota interval gave him, however, the Plains flavor crucial to the myth of Dorothy and the Wizard; gray desolation and hardscrabble rural survival compose the negative of which Oz is the colorful print. In Baum's Kansas, "even the grass was not green, for the sun had burned the tops of the long blades until they were the same gray color to be seen everywhere." Chicago's spectacular White City, built of plaster and cement for the 1893 World's Columbian Exposition on the lakeside marshes, gave both Baum and his illustrator, Denslow, the glitz and scale, but not the tint, of Oz's Emerald City. A contemporary writer, Frances Hodgson Burnett, likened the White City to the City Beautiful in Bunyan's *Pilgrim's Progress*, and wrote:

> Endless chains of jewels seemed strung and wound about it. The Palace of Flowers held up a great crystal of light glowing against the dark blue of the sky, towers and domes were crowned and diademed, thousands of jewels hung among the masses of leaves, or reflected themselves, sparkling in the darkness of the lagoons, fountains of molten jewels sprung up, and flamed and changed.

Woven of electric illusion (newly feasible, thanks to the Wizard of Menlo Park) and quickly an abandoned ruin, the White City fed into Baum's book a melancholy undertone of insubstantiality. A Bobbs-Merrill press release in 1903 claimed that the name Oz came from the "O-Z" drawer of the author's filing cabinet, but the name resonates with a Shelley poem known to most Victorians:

> And on the pedestal these words appear:
> "My name is Ozymandias, king of kings:
> Look on my works, ye Mighty, and despair!"
> Nothing beside remains.

A note of hollowness, of dazzling fraud, of frontier fustian and quackery taints the Wizard in the first of the many Oz books, before a plethora of wonders turns him into a real sorcerer. In the M-G-M movie, the seekers along the yellow brick road rapturously sing, "The Wizard of Oz is one because . . . because of the wonderful things he does"; then it turns out that what he does is concoct visual hokum with a crank and escape in a mismanaged hot-air balloon.

But Baum, who turned to editing and writing as a way of spending more time with his four young sons, proved to be an authentic wizard as a children's author. He had made the acquaintance of William Wallace Denslow, a footloose artist from Philadelphia who had come to Chicago for the Exposition; the two had definite and ambitious ideas about what children's books should look like, and paid for the color plates of their first collaboration, a book of Baum's verses called *Father Goose, His Book*. The book attracted praise from Mark Twain, William Dean Howells, and Admiral George Dewey and, Hearn says, "became the best-selling picture book of 1900" That year saw the publication of no fewer than five titles by Baum, of which the *Wizard* was the last. Hill was overwhelmed by orders, and went back to press four times, for a total of ninety thousand copies. The Minneapolis *Journal* called it, in November, "the best children's story-book of the century"—high praise if the nineteenth century was meant, more modest if the infant twentieth.

In 1902, the George M. Hill Company went bankrupt, in spite of Baum's success, and the rights to the *Wizard* were placed in the crasser hands of Bobbs-Merrill; meanwhile, Baum and Denslow parted, each taking the Oz characters with him, since their contract provided for separate ownership of text and illustrations. That same year saw the opening, at Chicago's Grand Opera House, of *The Wizard of Oz*, a "musical extravaganza" created by Julian Mitchell, who was later to mastermind *The Ziegfeld Follies*. Mitchell, had scrawled "No Good" across Baum's script for a five-act operetta closely based on his tale, and substituted a vaudevillian hodgepodge that capped its Chicago success with a year-and-a-half run on Broadway and a road career that lasted, off and on, until 1911. The extravaganza increased Baum's wealth, but it also encouraged his tropism toward the theatrical. His first sequel to the *Wizard*, *The Marvelous Land of Oz*, in 1904, was designed to be the basis of another extravaganza, featuring the vaudeville performers David C. Montgomery and Fred A. Stone, who had played the Tin Woodman and the Scarecrow in the Mitchell production. The book was dedicated to them and loaded with patter and puns suitable to their routines. It sold as a book but failed as a musical called *The Woggle-Bug*, with lyrics by Baum and without, in the end, Montgomery and Stone. Anticipating the piggyback publicity system perfected by

Walt Disney, Baum promoted this unfortunate production with a "Woggle-Bug Contest" in a Sunday comic page, drawn by Walt McDougall and titled "Queer Visitors from the Marvelous Land of Oz."

Despite frail health (angina, gallstones, inflamed appendix), Baum was a whirlwind of activity until his death, at the age of sixty-two. Along with thirteen Oz sequels, he wrote a teen-age-oriented *Aunt Jane's Nieces* series under the name Edith Van Dyne, young people's books under four other pseudonyms, an adult novel published anonymously, and many unpublished plays. Splendidly dressed in a white frock coat with silk lapels, he toured with film-and-slide presentations called "The Fairylogue and Radio-Plays." A reviewer in the Chicago *Tribune* wrote that "his ability to hold a large audience's attention during two hours of tenuous entertainment was amply demonstrated"; these early electronic productions were expensive, however, and by 1911 had helped bankrupt him. Thriftily moving his California winter residence from the Hotel del Coronado to a "handsome bungalow he christened Ozcot," in Hollywood, Baum found himself surrounded by the burgeoning movie industry without being able to tap into it profitably. The Oz Film Manufacturing Company, with Baum as president, produced some silent films, beginning with *The Patchwork Girl of Oz* in 1914, but, dismissed as "kiddie shows," they fell short at the box office. In 1925, six years after Baum's death, a movie of *The Wizard of Oz* was released; according to Hearn in one of his sterner moods, it was "totally lacking the magic of Baum's book" (though a Laurel-less Oliver Hardy played the Tin Woodman), and "had a dreadful script, written in part by the author's son Frank J. Baum." It was M-G-M's 1939 adaptation, of course, that hit the jackpot: the three-million-dollar film showed no profit on its original release, but it became a staple of postwar television. A hundred years after the *Wizard*'s publication, the movie is the main road into Oz.

Oz had very quickly become zoned for commercial activity, and there is something depressing about the chronicle of its exploitation, a chronicle that Hearn caps with a compendious footnote taking us up through the all-black *Wiz* (stage 1975, movie 1978) and the dead-on-arrival Disney *Return to Oz* (1985). And then there is the upcoming television series *Lost in Oz*, produced by Tim Burton. It is hard to read Baum's later Oz books without feeling the exploitation in progress, by a writer who only dimly understands his own masterpiece. After his death, the series was extended by Ruth Plumly Thompson, who between 1921 and 1939 added nineteen titles; then, briefly, by John R. Neill, whose spidery, often insipid drawings illustrate all the Oz books but the first; by Jack Snow, a "minor science fiction writer"; by Rachel Cosgrove; by Eloise Jarvis McGraw and Lauren McGraw Wagner; and even by Baum's son, who legally battled his mother for the precious trademark "Oz." And, Hearn indefatigably tells us, "of late there has grown up a peculiar literary sub-genre of adult novels drawing on the Oz mythology," such as Geoff Ryman's *Was* (1992) and Gregory Maguire's *Wicked: The Life and Times of the Wicked Witch of the West* (1995)—the products, presumably, of Oz-besotted children now aged into postmodern creators freed from fear of copyright infringement.

The potent images of the *Wizard* do cry out for extension and elaboration. The M-G-M motion picture improves upon the book in a number of ways. It eliminates, for example, the all too Aesopian (and, prior to computer graphics, probably unfilmable) episode wherein the Queen of the mice and her many minions transport the Cowardly Lion out of the poppy bed where he has fallen asleep; instead, it retrieves from the 1902 musical the effective stage business that had a sudden snowstorm annul the spell of the poppies. The movie weeds out a number of extravagant beasts and the especially artificial episode of "the Dainty China Country" so quaintly planted on the path to the witch's lair. The scenario amplifies the role of the Wicked Witch of the West, showing her as the source of all the obstacles in the pilgrims' path, as she watches them on the private television of her crystal ball. In the book, she is a relatively passive presence, easily doused ("I never thought a little girl like you would ever be able to melt me and end my wicked deeds. Look out—here I go!"), compared with the crackling green-faced film presence of Margaret Hamilton, who dies mourning her "beautiful wickedness!" Once she is dead, the film picks up speed; after the Wizard's unmasking and his unplanned departure, it is virtually over, where Baum's tale dillydallies through further complications on the way to the Good Witch of the South, with fresh humanoid gadgetry like Fighting Trees and armless Hammer-Heads and a mechanical plot dependency on the Golden Cap and its three-wish control of the Winged Monkeys. As a writer, Baum rarely knew when to quit, unfurling marvel after marvel while the human content—a content shaped by nonmagical limitations—leaked away. He did not quite grasp that his *Wizard* concerns our ability to survive disillusion; miracles are humbug.

The Hollywood film begins with the human, gray Kansas and, unlike the book, plants on that drab land all the actors who will dominate Oz—the three farmhands, the wicked Almira Gulch on her bicycle, Professor Marvel in his flimsy van. They are Kansans, and Dorothy returns to them. Hearn calls it "unforgivable" that the M-G-M movie cast Oz as a dream; but Dorothy on awakening protests, "It wasn't a dream." It was an alternative reality, an inner depiction of how we grow. As Jerome Charyn observes in his excellent *Movieland: Hollywood and the Great American Dream Culture* (1989), "The whole film was about metamorphosis." Judy Garland, who was sixteen and noticeably buxom in the role of Baum's prepubescent Dorothy, was "a woman who seemed to flower from an ordinary little girl." Growth is metamorphosis, and self-understanding is growth. The Scarecrow already has brains, the Tin Woodman is sentimental to a fault, the Lion has courage enough, but until the Wizard bestows external evidences (in the movie more wittily than in the book) they feel deficient. Dorothy, capable and clear-sighted from the start, needs only to accept the grayness of home as a precious color, and to wish to return as ardently as she wish to escape "Over the Rainbow"—the movie's grand theme song, nearly removed from the final cut.

Like Charyn and Salman Rushdie (who has extolled the *Wizard* as "a parable of the migrant condition"), I belong to the generation more affected by the movie than by the book. For the testimony of one who read all the Oz books with adolescent credulity and delight, Gore Vidal's long essay of 1977, printed in two parts in *The New York Review of Books*, is impressive and peppery. He sees Baum as a protester against the violence of the rising American empire and "the iron Puritan order." It is true that an undercurrent of dissidence in the Oz books seems to have antagonized some librarians and critics; the director of the Detroit Library System, Ralph Ulveling, in 1957 pronounced them guilty of "negativism" and "a cowardly approach to life." Baum, in his introduction to the *Wizard*, strikes a challenging note; he deplores the "horrible and blood-curdling" incidents contained in "the old-time fairy tale" and promises his readers "a modernized fairy tale, in which the wonderment and joy are retained and the heart-aches and nightmares are left out." American Theosophy, to which Baum had been introduced by his formidable mother-in-law, mixed spiritualism and Buddhist and Hindu beliefs with a meliorism that rejected the darker, Devil-acknowledging side of Christianity. "God is Nature, and Nature God," Baum said; yet he also professed an animistic vision in which

> every bit of wood, every drop of liquid, every grain of sand or portion of rock has its myriads of inhabitants. . . . These invisible and vapory beings are known as Elementals. . . . They are soulless, but immortal; frequently possessed of extraordinary intelligence, and again remarkably stupid.

Madame H. P. Blavatsky, founder of the Theosophical Society, in her book *Isis Unveiled* (1878) wrote of these

Elementals as "the creatures evolved in the four kingdoms of earth, air, fire, and water, and called by the kabalists gnomes, sylphs, salamanders, and undines." This giddying, virtually bacterial multitudinousness came to characterize Oz as sequels multiplied its regions and its strange and magical tribes; but the *Wizard* itself presents an uncluttered cosmogony, drawn in bright blunt tints. According to Theosophy, our astral bodies come in distinct colors, and so do the regions of Oz, with their inhabitants. As Vidal points out, Oz exists in orderly patches like the extensive gardens that Baum remembered from his childhood home, and which he recreated in the geometrical plots of his garden at Ozcot.

The evils of capitalism, whose rewards proved so fickle for Baum, are absent from his alternative world. Enemies of socialism find in "The Emerald City" this much quoted passage:

> There were no poor people . . . because there was no such thing as money, and all property of every sort belonged to the Ruler. The people were her children, and she [Princess Ozma] cared for them. Each person was given freely by his neighbors whatever he required for his use, which is as much as anyone may reasonably desire.

But the proletariat does not rule; rather, it is ruled in a mock-medieval manner, by benevolent tyrants more often than not female, in keeping, perhaps, with the feminist tendencies of Theosophy and Matilda Gage's militant suffrag-

THE WONDERFUL WIZARD OF OZ

ism. Baum's rulers have a parental absolutism: Glinda is the ideal, ever-resourceful mother and the Wizard a typically bumbling father in Oz's sitcom as Baum first conceived it. Though he supported the populist William Jennings Bryan in 1896 and 1900, and the literature of the late nineteenth century abounds in literary Utopias, Oz is too unearthly to carry much political punch. It is constructed not of revolutionary intent but of wishful thinking. What earthiness the *Wizard* does have derives in considerable part from Denslow's sturdy, antic illustrations. Denslow, we learn in Hearn's *Annotated Wizard*, sometimes operated independently of the text: he drew a bear where Baum mentions a tiger, crowns the Lion before the author does, dresses Dorothy in her old gingham frock when Baum still has her in her Emerald City silks, and consistently omits (as does the movie) the "round, shining mark" that the Good Witch of the North plants, as protection, on her forehead with a kiss.

A centennial is a time for praise, but this reader is inclined to accept the invitation to argue with Hearn when he states, "Arguably there have been three great classic quests in American literature, Herman Melville's *Moby-Dick; or The Whale* (1851), Mark Twain's *Adventures of Huckleberry Finn* (1883), and L. Frank Baum's *The Wonderful Wizard of Oz* (1900)." Whatever their flaws of carelessness or aesthetic miscalculation, the first two titles were gloriously *written*, in the ambition of telling all the truth, "heart-aches and nightmares" included. *The Wizard* is relatively a lucky bauble, in the flat clear style of a man giving dictation. Nor does it seem to me true that "Uncle Henry and Aunt Em have come to symbolize the stern American farmer and his wife as much as the couple in Grant Wood's famous painting *American Gothic* have." Hearn has been too long peering through the magnifying glass of *The Baum Bugle*, the triquarterly publication of the International Wizard of Oz Club, "founded in 1957 by thirteen-year-old Justin G. Schiller." In the course of his devotedly researched footnotes, Hearn sometimes nods into critical banality: "Much of the charm and wit of *The Wizard of Oz* relies on Baum's irony and amusing incongruity"; the Cowardly Lion "proves Ernest Hemingway's dictum that courage is grace under pressure." A juster analogy, drawn by Hearn more than once, is with *The Pilgrim's Progress*, another few-frills picaresque search story by an author in his forties with a habit of public performance (Bunyan was a preacher). The *Wizard* is a *Pilgrim's Progress* emptied of religion, except for the Theosophist inkling that there are many universes. At a time when children's literature was still drenched in what Hearn calls "the putrid Puritan morality of the Sunday schools," Baum produced a refreshingly agnostic fantasy. The witches are too comically wicked to be evil. The humbug Wizard, accused by Dorothy of being "a very bad man," protests, "I'm really a very good man; but I'm a very bad Wizard, I must admit." In another bold stroke of American simplification, Baum invented escapism without escape. Dorothy opts to forsake Oz; gray, windswept Kansas is reinstated (less thumpingly than in the movie) as the seat of lasting, familial happiness. Indeed, as a practical matter it is easier to color with contentment the place where we are than to find a Technicolor paradise. Denslow's last drawing shows the return with more exuberance than

Baum's prose manages. In her hurry, little Dorothy runs so hard that her silver shoes, Baum's less photogenic original of M-G-M's glistening ruby slippers, are flying off; we feel her rounding the bases (Scarecrow, Tin Woodman, Cowardly Lion) to home plate.

L. Frank Baum and his trusty typewriter, taken at The Sign of the Goose, his lake house at Macatawa Park, Michigan.

THE FATHER OF THE WIZARD OF OZ

by Daniel P. Mannix

A t the turn of the century, a disillusioned man who had failed at almost everything he had attempted wrote to his sister: "When I was young I longed to write a great novel that should win me fame. Now that I am getting old my first book is written to amuse children. For, aside from my evident inability to do anything 'great,' I have learned to regard fame as a will-o-the-wisp ... but to please a child is a sweet and lovely thing that warms one's heart."

The man was Lyman Frank Baum, and his best-known book began to take form when a group of children, led by his own four boys, waylaid him one evening in his modest Chicago home, demanding a story. After a hard day's work, Baum often turned to fantasy as many men turn to alcohol.

Sitting down with the children surrounding him, he began to talk. He gave no thought to what he was saying and later wrote in amazement, "The characters surprised even me—it was as though they were living people." Baum told of a little Kansas farm girl named Dorothy who was carried by a cyclone to a strange land where she met a live scarecrow, a man made of tin, and a cowardly lion. One of the children asked, "What was the name of this land, Mr. Baum?" Stumped, Baum looked around him for inspiration. In the next room were filing cabinets, and one bore the letters O-Z. "The land of Oz!" exclaimed the storyteller and continued with the tale, unaware that he had added a new word to the English language.

Baum seldom bothered to write down his stories, but he was strangely attracted to this tale. After the children had gone, he went to his desk, pulled out a handful of scrap paper, and jotted it down. The next day, he took his collection of notes to W. W. Denslow, a hard-bitten newspaper artist with whom he had collaborated on an earlier juvenile, *Father Goose: His Book*.

The two men could not have been more different. Baum was shy, delicate in health, and unsophisticated about money. Denslow was aggressive, aspiring, and a heavy drinker; a lady once called him "a delightful old reprobate who looked like a walrus." Denslow outlined an ambitious program for the proposed book—twenty-four of his drawings as full-page illustrations in a six-color printing scheme and innumerable sketches tinted in various tones to be superimposed on the text. Baum eagerly agreed to everything.

Publishers did not. The two men were turned down by nearly every house in Chicago. Baum's conception of an "American fairy story" was too radical a departure from traditional juvenile literature, and Denslow's elaborate illustrations would price the book off the market. At last, George Hill agreed to publish the book according to Denslow's plan, provided Baum and Denslow would pay all printing expenses. The two men turned their royalties from *Father Goose* over to Hill, who thought the new book "might sell as much as 5,000 copies."

It was called *The Wonderful Wizard of Oz* and was published on August 1, 1900. By October, twenty-five thousand more copies had to be printed, and thirty thousand more in November—and all this through word-of-mouth advertising Hill, who had put most of the firm's resources into good, reliable books with a "sure sale" (the majority of which were remaindered), was totally unprepared for such a phenomenon. Unable to believe this fairy tale was really a best seller, he refused to push it until too late. His company failed while he was still trying to rush copies of the *Wizard* off the presses.

But another publisher snapped up the book and it continued to sell. Today, over five million copies of *The Wonderful Wizard of Oz* have been published, making it one of the great best sellers of all time. It has been made into musical comedies, silent and sound movies, puppet shows, radio shows, and LP records. The 1939 MGM Technicolor musical with Judy Garland is now shown on television every Christmas, a recognized American tradition. Judy has sung "Over the Rainbow" more times than anyone can count. There have been some thirty editions of the *Wizard*, and over ten are in print now. A first edition sold in 1962 for $875, another with an inscription by Baum went for $3,500. It has been translated into over a dozen foreign languages and in Russia is being used to teach school children English. A nice Russian touch: the Munchkins (the little people who first meet Dorothy when she arrives in Oz) are described as the Chewing People, the Russian experts reasonably arguing that to munch means to chew. But my own favorite is the Chinese version, in which the Cowardly Lion looks like a very cheerful dragon.

Two years after the *Wizard*'s success, a Broadway producer named Julian Mitchell conceived the idea of doing the book as a musical extravaganza—quite as fantastic a notion as Baum's original inspiration. Delighted, Baum wrote the script, keeping strictly to the book's story line, but Mitchell had a few ideas of his own. The play as it finally appeared featured a chorus in the standard "beef trust" tradition; Dorothy's little dog Toto was transformed into a comic cow named Imogene; and Dorothy herself, a hefty soubrette, fell in love with a "Poet Prince" in the grand finale. But the cast also included two unknown but talented comics: Dave Montgomery as the Tin Woodman and Fred Stone as the Scarecrow. Within weeks, Montgomery and Stone became the best-known comic team in America. Baum protested Mitchell's innovations, but when the play ran nearly ten years and earned him some $100,000 in royalties (then a huge sum), he published a letter apologizing to the producer. "People will have what pleases them," wrote Baum philosophically.

The life of Lyman Frank Baum—he always used the initial L because he considered "Lyman" affected—was nearly as bizarre as those of his Oz characters. His father, Benjamin Baum, was a hard-driving oil man of German ancestry. He dared oppose the formidable Standard Oil Company and won at least a partial victory in the Pennsylvania oil fields. (In *Sea Fairies*, Baum describes an octopus bursting into tears on being compared to the Standard Oil Company.) Benjamin Baum made a comfortable fortune and settled on a large estate at Chittenango, near Syracuse, New York. Here Frank Baum was born May 15, 1856, the seventh of nine children. His mother, Cynthia Stanton Baum, was of Scotch-Irish descent and a strict Episcopalian. She would not even allow the children to play baseball on Sunday and filled the house with learned, solemn individuals whom Baum later caricatured in the person of H. M. Woggle-Bug, T. E. (Highly Magnified and Thoroughly Educated).

Frank Baum was a shy, sickly child. Unable to play games with the other boys, he spent most of his time acting out fantasies with a host of imaginary playmates created by giving personalities to everything from his mechanical toys to the chickens he loved to feed. One of these chickens appears in the Oz books as Billina. Once during a walk the boy saw a scarecrow and was terrified by the strange man-like creature. For months afterward, he repeatedly dreamed that it was chasing him. The dream was so vivid that he could later distinctly recall the phantom's ungainly lope, his lack of co-ordination, and his final collapse into a heap of straw. That this ogre could ever change into the beloved, friendly scarecrow of the Oz books seems incredible, but one of Baum's great talents was the ability to transform a bête noire into an amusing, sympathetic personality.

When Baum was twelve, his parents decided that the sentimental boy needed to be shaken out of his dream world. He was sent to the Peekskill Military Academy. The tough discipline was too much for the delicate youngster, and he had a nervous breakdown. From then on he was educated by private tutors. Baum was always to dislike the military. A favorite theme in the Oz books is the overstaffed army, composed of hordes of generals, colonels, majors, and captains commanding one browbeaten private who is expected to do all the fighting. But Baum was never capable of real hatred: even the officers are affectionately described. A general's explanation for his abject cowardice is the reasonable statement that "Fighting is unkind and liable to be injurious to others."

Naturally enough, the imaginative young man became enamored of the stage and, with money supplied by his father, started a Shakespearean troupe. By his own admission the only successful performance occurred when the ghost of Hamlet's father fell through a hole in the stage. The audience, which happened to be composed of oil workers, was so delighted that the unhappy ghost had to repeat the stunt five times. Baum also tried his hand at playwriting, and one of his plays, *The Maid of Arran*, was a great success with audiences of immigrant Irish because of its sentimental picture of Ireland. Through his mother Baum had developed a highly romantic conception of the Emerald Isle, which may explain why the heart of Oz is called the Emerald City.

Returning home from one of his tours, Baum met a

twenty-year-old girl named Maud Gage, daughter of the militant suffragette Matilda Joslyn Gage. The young couple instantly fell in love—possibly because they were so different. The gentle Baum admired the girl's bold outlook, and Maud felt a motherly interest in the eager young dreamer. Also, Baum was an unusually handsome man, slightly over six feet with wavy brown hair and a delightful twinkle in his eye. Mrs. Gage violently opposed the marriage, regarding Baum as hopelessly impractical, but in her resolute daughter the strong-minded old lady met her match. There was a stormy scene between the two, while the prospective bridegroom stood by helplessly. The couple were married in 1881.

Soon there was a baby son, and with a family to support, Baum left the theatre and went into his family's petroleum-products business. For a while he sold Baum's Castorine, a patented axle grease. But in 1887 Benjamin Baum was severely injured in an accident, and without the astute old man's guiding hand the business failed.

It was Maud who rallied from the blow and kept the family going. The Baums had two sons now and had salvaged only a few thousand dollars from the wreck of the family fortune. From Aberdeen, South Dakota, where a gold rush was raging, Maud's brother wrote that there were unlimited opportunities for anyone who would open a small store for the gold seekers. So the Baums went to Aberdeen and started a shop called Baum's Bazaar. Maud's brother had been almost right; it was impossible for anyone to fail in a gold rush town—anyone, that is, except L. Frank Baum. He did it by refusing to accept money from those who were destitute. His habit of ignoring customers to sit on the curb outside the store telling stories to groups of enthralled children didn't do the business any good either. In two years, he had 161 strictly nonpaying clients and the bazaar went bankrupt.

Baum then started a newspaper called *The Aberdeen Saturday Pioneer*, setting the type himself and doing most of the writing, including a special column called "Our Landlady." This was a fantasy describing a community where people rode in "horseless carriages" (the first American automobile had not yet gone on sale) or flying machines, did their dishes in mechanical dishwashers, slept under electric blankets, and ate concentrated foods. The cattle were fed wood shavings, having been fitted with green glasses that made the shavings look like grass. (In the Emerald City, everything looks green to the inhabitants, even the sky. The Wizard achieves this magical effect by requiring everyone to wear green-tinted spectacles.) In spite of the prophetic element in these tales, they are told simply as burlesque—or as Baum would have put it, "banter." Neither he nor his readers took such ideas seriously, and the stories resemble the typical "tall tales" of the West more than they do science fiction.

In the tradition of western newspapermen of that period, Baum made a brave attempt to turn his talent for satire against rival editors. He succeeded so well that he found himself challenged to a duel by an enraged subscriber. The two men, each with a revolver low-slung on the hip, were to walk around the town until they met and then shoot it out in now-familiar Grade B movie style. In this crisis, Frank Baum was magnificent. All his latent sense of the dramatic came to the fore, and he made an imposing picture as he strode off from his doorway, while passers-by took refuge behind the false fronts of nearby buildings. But as soon as he had turned the corner, Baum, like his Oz general, decided that fighting was unkind and someone was likely to be hurt. He quietly disappeared until the affair blew over.

Maud Baum had her third son in Aberdeen. The father was so sure the child would be a girl that he had even picked the name Geraldine for the baby. He desperately wanted a little girl, and Mrs. Baum made one more attempt to oblige. Alas, a fourth son arrived, and Frank Baum was never to have the little daughter he so greatly craved.

In 1891 the *Pioneer* failed, or as Baum put it, "I decided the sheriff wanted the paper more than I did." The family left for Chicago. Baum had no regrets in leaving South Dakota and the great, barren prairie. A passage in the *Wizard* was to describe his feelings toward it: "Dorothy could see nothing but the great gray prairie on every side. Not a tree nor a house broke the broad sweep of flat country that reached the edge of the sky in all directions. The sun had baked the plowed land into a gray mass, with little cracks running through it. Even the grass was not green, for the sun burned the tops of the long blades until they were the same gray color to be seen everywhere." Dorothy escapes from this bleak, colorless land to the cool green hills, soft shadows, and clear, fresh streams of Oz, which bore a strong resemblance to the Baum family estate in Chittenango.

But Chicago was not Chittenango. Baum got a job as a reporter for twenty dollars a week, and the family moved into a wretched house with no bathroom or running water.

Maud gave embroidery lessons at ten cents an hour. When Baum's salary was cut to $18.62, he left his job with the paper and became a travelling salesman for a crockery firm. About the only recreation the four boys had was to listen to their father's fairy stories, in which Baum himself became so lost that his wife once said rather unhappily, "I honestly don't believe he can tell truth from fancy." These tales were his escape from his miserable existence.

Then Mrs. Gage, Maud's mother, moved in with them. Baum and his mother-in-law had never gotten along well, but he should have been everlastingly grateful to the old lady for one contribution: listening to his stories, Mrs. Gage ordered, "You go out and have those published." Baum laughed at the idea but his wife said firmly, "Mother is nearly always right about everything." Nagged by the two women, Baum sent out a collection of stories suggested by the Mother Goose rhymes, which was published in 1897 under the title, *Mother Goose in Prose*. The illustrator was an unknown young artist named Maxfield Parrish. It was a "first" for both of them. The book did sufficiently well for the publishers to ask for another, so Baum wrote the *Father Goose* sequel, this time with Denslow as illustrator. Then came the miraculous success of the *Wizard*.

When Baum was possessed by his fantasies, he wandered around in a trance. "His best friends could speak to him at such times and he wouldn't recognize them," Mrs. Baum recalled. His characters were intensely real to him. Once when he had not written for several weeks, his wife asked him what was the matter. "My characters won't do what I want them to," replied Baum irritably. A few days later he was back at work. Maud Baum asked him how he had solved the problem. "By letting them do what they want to do," her husband explained. An ardent naturalist, he never hunted, feeling, like the Tin Woodman, that killing animals was cruel. Ozma, the Ruler of Oz, says firmly, "No one has the right to kill any living creature, however evil they may be, or to hurt them, or make them unhappy."

The format of the *Wizard* is simple. As Baum says in his introduction, he desired to eliminate "all the horrible and blood-curdling incidents" of the old-time fairy tales. He adhered to this principle in all his Oz books. Dorothy melts the Wicked Witch of the West with a bucket of water, but unlike the witch in Grimm's *Snow White*, she is not strapped into red-hot iron shoes and forced to dance until she dies. The Nome King (Baum believed that "gnome" was too difficult for a child to pronounce) threatens to turn Dorothy into a piece of bric-a-brac but does not plan to ravish her, skin her feet, and bind her toes so they will grow together, as in George MacDonald's *The Princess and the Goblin*. The late James Thurber said he had suffered agonies as a child when the Sawhorse, in *The Marvelous Land of Oz*, broke his leg; but the injury did not hurt the horse, nor was the animal put into a furnace and reduced to a little heart-shaped lump while his sweetheart looked on, as in Andersen's *The Steadfast Tin Soldier*. As Robert Louis Stevenson was able to make the dialogue of his pirates seem brutal and coarse without ever using an oath, Baum managed to make his villains threatening without going into specific and horrendous detail, at the same time deftly maintaining suspense and an atmosphere of peril.

Baum also hoped to eliminate the "stereotyped genie, dwarf and fairy." Here again he was remarkably successful. Like all his characters, the Scarecrow, the Tin Woodman, and the Cowardly Lion are distinct personalities; children learn to know them, become genuinely interested in them, and feel concern over their fates.

Dorothy was perhaps Baum's most successful creation. Unlike the immortal Alice, who wanders politely through Wonderland without trying to influence events, Dorothy—although always gentle and innocent—is a quietly determined little girl. She intends to get back to her aunt and uncle, and neither the Great and Terrible Oz nor a wicked witch is going to prevent her. She is undoubtedly the leader of the little group of adventurers; though she turns to the Woodman for comfort, the Scarecrow for advice, and the Lion for protection, they would obviously be lost without her. Dorothy is the descendant of the pioneer women who crossed the plains and the grandmother of every soap-opera heroine who ever faced life. She is as American as Alice is Victorian British.

Most amazing of all was Baum's ability to make Oz a real place. Any child suddenly transported there would instantly recognize the country. It can even be mapped, and has been several times. Baum achieves this effect partly by precise details (there are 9,654 buildings in the Emerald City and the population is 57,318) but mainly by extraordinarily vivid descriptions of the forests, the poppy fields, the rivers, and the winding Road of Yellow Brick.

Baum carried into his own life his peculiar talent of making the unbelievable believable. He was forbidden to smoke because of his heart condition, but he often held a large, unlighted cigar in his mouth. The poet Eunice Tietjens, visiting the Baums at their home in Macatawa on the shore of Lake Michigan, asked why he never lighted the cigar. Baum explained that he did so only when he went swimming. "You see," he explained gravely, "I can't swim, so when the cigar goes out I know I'm getting over my depth." Then he lighted the cigar and walked into the lake until the cigar was extinguished. "There now," Baum said when he returned to land, "if it hadn't been for the cigar I would have drowned."

Baum loved to recount some matter-of-fact event and then embroider it with increasingly grotesque details while maintaining a perfectly serious attitude. The game was to see how far he could go before his listeners realized he was joking. He could fool even his own family, who of course knew the trick. Once he was telling his serious-minded mother a fantastic tale which deceived her for a long time, until she finally caught on and said severely, "Frank, you are telling a story." Her son replied, "Well, mother, as you know, in St. Paul's Epistle to the Ephesians, he said 'all men are liars.' " His bewildered mother, saying, "I don't recall that," got her Bible and began to search until she suddenly realized she had been tricked again.

Delighted as he was by the success of the *Wizard*, Baum had no intention of writing another Oz book. Convinced that he had found the perfect formula for writing fairy tales, he followed the *Wizard* with *Dot and Trot of Merryland*, *American Fairy Tales*, and *The Master Key*, the last a science-fiction story with philosophical overtones. They had only a moderate success. He then tried *The Life and Adventures of Santa Claus*, which many consider a far better work than the Oz books. Unfortunately for Baum, the children didn't agree. He then wrote *The Enchanted Island of Yew*, a story more in the old European tradition. It had only a modest sale. To children, Oz was a real place. These other stories were only "fairy tales."

Shortly after the success of the *Wizard*, Baum had jokingly told a little girl—who was also a Dorothy—that if a thousand little girls wrote him asking for a sequel he would write one. At the moment, that hardly seemed likely, but he got the thousand letters and more. At last, in 1904, he wrote *The Marvelous Land of Oz*, dedicating it to the two comics, Montgomery and Stone. Three new Oz characters appear who were to become famous: Jack Pumpkinhead, the Sawhorse and H. M. Woggle-Bug. Part of the book is a satire on the suffragette movement, but a cheerful one. The pretty General Jinjur defeats the army of the Emerald City by waving a knitting needle but is panic-stricken when the Scarecrow releases some mice from his stuffed bosom. The hero of the book is Tip, a boy who is later transformed into a sweet young girl—Ozma, rightful ruler of Oz. *The Land of Oz* is the only Oz book in which Dorothy does not appear. Baum had a special feeling for her and at first resisted making Dorothy part of a routine series.

By 1904 Denslow and Baum had had a falling-out, and for this second Oz adventure the publishers hired a new artist, a twenty-five-year-old Philadelphian named John R. Neill. Neill's illustrations would become as closely identified with Baum as Tenniel's with Lewis Carroll, or Shepard's with A. A. Milne. Neill made Dorothy a pretty, slender girl instead of Denslow's dumpy farm child, and transformed Toto from a nondescript cur to a Boston bull. Denslow bitterly resented Neill's changes, but the younger man had a quiet revenge. In *The Road to Oz*, Dorothy visits the castle of the Tin Woodman, who has erected statues of his friends in the garden. Neill drew the statues in Denslow's style and showed his own Dorothy and Toto looking with amazement and amusement at their former selves. To stress the point, he drew Denslow's trademark, a seahorse, on the bases of the statues.

The Land of Oz was nearly as great a success as the *Wizard*, although the children missed Dorothy and wrote Baum hundreds of letters protesting her omission. Baum again tried to do other books. He wrote *Queen Zixi of Ix*, a beautifully plotted fairy tale; *John Dough and the Cherub*, about the adventures of a gingerbread man; and three adult novels which were unhappy mixtures of Anthony Hope and H. Rider Haggard. At last, in 1907, financial pressures forced him to write *Ozma of Oz*. Here Dorothy returns with Billina, the yellow hen, to rescue the royal family of Ev from Ruggedo, the Nome King Ruggedo was Baum's most successful villain and turns up in book after book. The Cowardly Lion has a companion in the Hungry Tiger (who longs to eat fat babies but is forbidden by his conscience), and Tiktok, said to be one of the first robots in American literature, aids them. The success of *Ozma* was so great that Baum never again wrote an Oz book without Dorothy.

In his next tale, *Dorothy and the Wizard in Oz*, Baum wrote ruefully, "It's no use, no use at all. I know lots of other stories but my loving tyrants won't allow me to tell them. They cry 'Oz—more about Oz!' " In this story, Dorothy and the Wizard are reunited when swallowed by an earthquake and work their way back to Oz via a series of underground kingdoms. With them are a farm boy named Jeb, a cab horse named Jim, and Eureka, Dorothy's pet kitten. As a bird lover, Baum didn't much like cats, and Eureka is a rather unpleasant personality, although Baum admired her independence, courage, and grace.

In *The Road to Oz*, Baum introduced Polychrome, the Rainbow's daughter; Button-Bright, who is always getting lost; and the Shaggy Man. In his search for realism, Baum used a curious device. There are four countries in Oz, each with its individual color, and as the characters move from one to another, the pages of the book change to the appropriate shade. Baum was still complaining, "I would like to write some stories that are not Oz stories," and at Ozma's birthday party, he introduces characters from his other books—Queen Zixi, John Dough, and King Bud of Noland—obviously in hopes of weaning children away from the land of the Wizard. Finally, in *The Emerald City of Oz*, Baum made a determined effort to bring the series to a halt. Although Oz is almost impossible to visit, because it is surrounded by the Deadly Desert (Baum liked to call it "the Shifting Sands"), Glinda, the Good Sorceress, now makes the country permanently invisible. The book ends with a letter from Dorothy, "You will never hear anything more about Oz because we are now cut off forever from the rest of the world. But Toto and I will always love you and all the other children who love us."

The panic that struck juvenile circles can only be compared to the consternation that hit London when Conan Doyle threw Sherlock Holmes off a cliff. For thousands of American youngsters, finding a new Oz book under the tree had become part of Christmas. A staff member at a children's hospital wrote Baum that the books were such a valuable morale booster that "they are as integral a part of our equipment as a thermometer." One of the most touching letters came from a mother whose little son had died of a lingering illness. "Only when I read your books to him could he forget his pain. As he died he told me, 'Now I will see the Princess of Oz.'" In spite of such heartbreaking entreaties, Baum refused to continue the series. Instead, he wrote two books about the adventures of Trot, a little California girl, and her companion, Cap'n Bill, an old one-legged sailor. In *Sea Fairies*, the two have adventures with mermaids and in *Sky Island* go to a land above the clouds. To make the stories more appealing Baum brought in some Oz characters.

It was no good. The children wanted nothing but Oz, and Baum was no longer his own master. He had invested heavily in "Radio Plays," hand-tinted transparencies designed to be shown by magic lantern in conjunction with motion pictures about Oz characters. (There was no connection with the radio, which had not yet been developed.) Baum was convinced that they would be a great success, but the process was too costly and the whole venture was a disaster. Several musicals that tried to duplicate the startling success of the *Wizard* failed also, partly because they lacked the magic of Montgomery and Stone. In 1911, Baum declared himself a bankrupt, listing his assets as "a five year old typewriter and two suits of clothing, one in actual use."

He had no choice now but to return to the Oz books. He wrote eight more, beginning with *The Patchwork Girl of Oz* in 1913. He was now living in Los Angeles and, delighted with the new motion pictures, made eager attempts to enter the field. Backed by such Hollywood notables as Will Rogers, George Arliss, Hal Roach, Harold Lloyd, and Darryl Zanuck, Baum started the Oz Film Manufacturing Company, on a seven-acre lot opposite the Universal Film Company. This venture also failed, and Maud Baum, with her usual quiet but determined efficiency, demanded that in the future all royalty checks should be made over to her. As a result the family remained solvent; Baum could no longer describe himself (as he had to one journalist asking for biographical information) as "constantly bent and occasionally broke."

Baum continued to turn out an Oz book a year, although he was suffering acute attacks of angina pectoris and his heart, never strong and now badly weakened by the strain of his repeated business failures, caused him constant trouble. Under such pen names as Floyd Akers, Laura Bancroft, Captain Hugh Fitzgerald, and Edith Van Dyne, he wrote a constant flow of juvenile novels, none of which even approximated the success of his fairy tales. The house he built near Sunset Boulevard he call Ozcot. Here he lived quietly, raising flowers and feeding the birds in his giant aviary. To children who came from all parts of the country to see the "Royal Historian of Oz" and listen to his stories, the house was a shrine. On May 5, 1919, he had a stroke, and died the next day. Maud Baum was with him to the end. His last words were, "Now we can cross the Shifting Sands."

Children could not believe he was dead. Even today Reilly & Lee, his publishers, get letters addressed to him. The Oz books were continued, first by a twenty-year-old Philadelphia girl named Ruth Plumly Thompson, then by John Neill, and afterward by Jack Snow, who took his work so seriously that he wrote a *Who's Who in Oz* giving the names of all Oz characters and a short biographical sketch of each. Rachel Cosgrove wrote one Oz book, and the series is now being continued by Eloise McGraw and Laurie Wagner. But Baum's originals still outsell their successors by six to one.

During Baum's lifetime and for many years after his death, his books were not taken seriously—except by the ever-enthusiastic children. Now even among grownups there is a constantly growing Oz cult. Baum devotees have formed the International Wizard of Oz Club, whose members collect everything they can find on Baum and learnedly debate such problems as why the Magic Powder of Life (which brings to life everything it touches) didn't animate its own container, and why Professor Woggle-Bug in his map of Oz put the Munchkin country to the west of the Emerald City when in the *Wizard* the Good Witch of the North says that it lies to the east. In the last thirty years the Baum books have been "discovered" by such notable persons as James Thurber, Phyllis McGinley, Philip Wylie, Clifton Fadiman, and, of all people, Dylan Thomas. Professor Russel B. Nye of Michigan State University, a Pulitzer Prize winner, and Professor Edward Wagenknecht of Boston University have published scholarly papers on Baum.

On the other hand, there has been a violent reaction

against him on the part of many librarians, child psychologists, and teachers. His books have been, from time to time, withdrawn from the shelves of public libraries. One librarian protested that the books were "untrue to life and consequently unwholesome for children," and another supported her, claiming that "Kids don't like that fanciful stuff any more. They want books about atomic missiles"—a cheerful prospect which is fortunately untrue: the Oz books continue to outsell almost all other juveniles. In Russia the story is given a slightly anti-American slant—for example, Dorothy lives in a Kansas trailer, and knows little about life because the American books she has are such shoddy productions—yet on the whole the Land of Oz has proved to be as inviolable behind the Iron Curtain as anywhere else. It is a unique tribute.

William Wallace Denslow, artist of *The Wonderful Wizard of Oz*.

Top: Photo of L. Frank Baum given to his wife, Maude. He wrote the following words on the back of it: "To my own Sweet Love. The image of your baby. Tooken [sic] December 1899."

Bottom: Maud Gage Baum in 1900.

BECAUSE, BECAUSE, BECAUSE, BECAUSE OF THE WONDERFUL THINGS HE DOES

by Ray Bradbury

Let us consider two authors whose books were burned in our American society during the past seventy years. Librarians and teachers did the burning very subtly by not buying. And not buying is as good as burning. Yet, the authors survived.

Two gentlemen of no talent whatsoever.

Two mysteries of literature, if you can call their work literature.

Two men who changed the world somewhat more than they ever dreamed, once they were in it, once their books came to be published and moved in the minds and blood of eight-year-olds, ten-year-olds, twelve-year-olds.

One of them changed the future of the entire world and

that Universe which waited for Earthmen to birth themselves in space with rockets.

His name: Edgar Rice Burroughs. His John Carter grew to maturity two generations of astronomers, geologists, biochemists, and astronauts who cut their teeth on his Barsoomian beasts and Martian fighting men and decided to grow up and grow out away from Earth.

The second man, also a "mediocre" talent, if you can believe the teachers and librarians of some seventy years, created a country, Oz, and peopled it with not one influence, but several dozens.

His name: L. Frank Baum.

And once you begin to name his people in his country, it is hard to stop: Dorothy, Toto (indeed a very real person), the Tin Man, the Scarecrow, Tik-Tok, Ozma, Polychrome, the Patchwork Girl, Ruggedo, Prof. Woggle-Bug, Aunty Em, the Wicked Witch of the—. You see how easily the names pop out, without having to go look them up!

Two mysteries, then. One the mystery of growing boys to men by romanticizing their taffy bones so the damn things *rise* toward the sun, no, toward Mars. Now, let us set Mr. Burroughs aside.

Let us get on with the mystery of L. Frank Baum, that faintly old-maidish man who grew boys inward to their most delightful interiors, kept them home, and romanced them with wonders between their ears.

And this book is, of course, about the latter mystery, the mystery of that strange dear little Wizard Himself. The man who wanted to work magic but, oh, dear, not *hurt* anyone along the way. He is that rare chef who would never dream to yell at his cooks, yet got results anyway: a bakery-kitchen full of valentines, sweet-meats, dragons without teeth, robots with feelings, Tin Men who were once real (to reverse the Pinocchio myth), and girls who are so toothsome and innocent that if you nibble them at all, it would only be their toes, ears, and elbows.

It is a book about a man compelled to money, but saved by his secret self, his hidden creative person.

It is a book about a man who set out, unknowingly, to slaughter his own best talents, but was saved by a mob of strange creatures from another land who knew better than he that they needed to be born. And in birthing themselves ensured the miraculous fact that if we all went to the nearest travel agency tomorrow and were asked if we wanted to go to Alice's Wonderland or the Emerald City, it would be that Green Place, and the Munchkins and the Quadlings and all the rest, every time.

It is fascinating to compare memories of Dorothy and Oz and Baum with Alice and the Looking Glass and the Rabbit Hole and Lewis Carroll, who made out better with librarians and teachers.

When we think of Oz a whole mob of incredibly lovely if strange people falls across our minds.

When we think of Alice's encounters we think of mean, waspish, small, carping, bad-mannered children ranting against *going* to bed, refusing to get *out* of bed, not liking the food, hating the temperature, minding the weather out of mind.

If Love is the lubricant that runs Oz to glory, Hate is the mud in which all sink to ruin inside the mirror where poor Alice is trapped.

If everyone goes around democratically accepting each other's foibles in the four lands surrounding the Emerald City, and feeling nothing but amiable wonder toward such eccentrics as pop up, the reverse is true when Alice meets a Caterpillar or Tweedledum and Tweedledee or assorted knights, Queens, and Old Women. Theirs is an aristocracy of snobs, no one is good enough for them. They themselves are crazy eccentrics, but eccentricity in anyone else is beyond comprehension and should best be guillotined or grown small and stepped on.

Both books, both authors, stay in our minds, for mirror-reversed reasons. We float and fly through Oz on grand winds that make us beautiful kites. We trudge and fight our way through Wonderland, amazed that we survive at all.

Wonderland, for all its fantasy, is most practically real, that world where people have conniption fits and knock you out of line on your way onto a bus.

Oz is that place, ten minutes before sleep, where we bind up our wounds, soak our feet, dream ourselves better, snooze poetry on our lips, and decide that mankind, for all it's snide and mean and dumb, must be given another chance come dawn and a hearty breakfast.

Oz is muffins and honey, summer vacations, and all the easy green time in the world.

Wonderland is cold gruel and arithmetic at six A.M., icy showers, long schools.

It is not surprising that Wonderland is the darling of the intellectuals.

It is similarly not surprising that dreamers and intuitionists would reject the cold mirror of Carroll and take their chances on hotfooting it over the forbidden desert which at least promises utter destruction for purely inanimate reasons (the desert, after all, is not alive and doesn't know whom it is destroying), heading for Oz. Because in Oz of course reside amiable villains who are really not villains at all. Ruggedo is a fraud and a sham, for all his shouts and leaping about and uttering curses. Whereas Wonderland's Queen of Hearts really *does* chop off heads and children are beaten if they sneeze.

Wonderland is what we Are.

Oz is what we would hope and like to be.

The distance between raw animal and improved human can be measured by pegging a line between Alice's Rabbit Hole and Dorothy's Yellow Brick Road.

One need not polarize oneself by picking one country, one heroine, one set of characters. It is not either-or, or this or that. It can be both.

It is the sad/happy state of mankind always to be making such measurements: where we are as against where we would like to be.

I hope that the lovers of Wonderland and the lovers of Oz do not break up into permanent warring camps. That would be foolish and fruitless, for growing humanity needs proper doses of reality and proper doses of dreaming. I would like to believe Alice puts antibodies in our blood to help us survive Reality by showing us as the fickle, reckless, abrupt, and alarming children we are. Children, of course, recognize themselves in the mostly bad-mannered grotesques that amble, stalk, and wander up to Alice.

But mean and loud and dreadful make for high tea lacking vitamins. Reality is an unsubstantial meal. Children also recognize a good dream when they see it, and so turn to Mr. Baum for the richer cake rather than the swamp gruel, for the mean-spirit that is really Santa Claus pretending at horrible. Children are willing to risk being smothered in true marmalade and saccharine. Mr. Baum provides both, with some narrow escapes from the maudlin and the thing we damn as sentimentality.

No matter if Mr. Baum was his own worst enemy . . . The more he tried to be commercial, the more his intuitive self seemed to pop to the surface saying, finally, "To hell with you, I'm going *my* way!" And away it went, dragging Mr. Baum screaming after it, he yelling for money, his Muse settling for warm creations. Ironically if Mr. B had relaxed more, and let the Muse drag him, he would probably have wound up wiser, happier, richer.

I suddenly realize . . . that a funny thing happened on my way into this Introduction: Mr. Carroll fell by and collided with Mr. Baum. In the resultant scramble, I was locked in and only now fight free.

What you have here, in the (book to which this is the Preface), is an attempt made by one of the first people, late in time, to pay attention to a spirited man with a nice old grandma's soul. It is an endeavor to "unburn" the histories of Oz, and shelve the Works where they have rarely, in the history of our country, been shelved: in libraries.

It is not the task of a writer of Prefaces to criticise or super-analyze the work at hand. If Raylyn Moore has done nothing else but begin to stir up some sort of small tempest concerning Oz and the super-evident fact it has stood, unassailed and beautific somewhere beyond Kansas for seventy-odd years, her task will have been commendable.

For Oz has not fallen, has it? Even though legions of bright people with grand good taste, and thousands of librarians have fired cannonades in tandem with hosts of sociologists who fear that the mighty Wizard will pollute their children, Baum, across the years, simply reaches in his pocket and produces, Shaggy Man that he is, the Love Magnet.

And if he is not the Shaggy Man, which he surely is, he is the Pied Piper who takes the adoring children away from their dull and unappreciative parents. Let the older folk survive into starvation with their algebra breakfasts, mathematical luncheons, and computer-data-fact dinners. To the children, Baum cries, "Let them eat cake!" but *means* it, and delivers.

In a story of mine published some twenty-two years ago, *The Exiles*, fine fantasists like Poe and Hawthorne, along with Dickens, and Baum, find themselves shunted off to Mars as the nondreamers, the super-psychological technicians, the book burners of the future, advance through towns and libraries, tossing the last of the great dreams into the furnace.

At the finale of my story, a rocket arrives on Mars, bearing with it the last copies in existence of Poe and Dickens and Baum. The captain of the ship burns these books on a dead Martian sea-bottom, and Oz at long last crashes over into ruins, Tik-Tok runs to rust, the Wizard and all his dusk-time dreams are destroyed, even as Scrooge, Marley, the Three Spirits, the Raven and the Masque of the Red Death fly away into dusks, gone forever.

I do not for a moment believe that day will ever come. The fight between the dreamers and the fact-finders will continue, and we will embody both in equal proportion, or risk all men singing *castrato* soprano for the literary popes.

I have not predicted futures but, as I have often hope-fully pointed out, prevented them. How much has my ounce counted for in a world of data dross?

Who can say? I only know that 1984 is not coming after all. For a while there we actually thought it might. Man as mere computer-adjunct data collector realist is losing to man as loving companion to a miraculous universe. By such hopes I must live.

Raylyn Moore, if I read her rightly, has given us a book here of such a size and weight as to knock librarians' heads with, and bang sociologists' elbows with, and knock psychi-atrists' hats askew. Whether she intends it or not, in sum here I believe her to say, in all truth:

Shakespeare invented Freud.

Hell, Shakespeare invented *everything!*

And long before the first couch was lain upon and the first psychiatrical confession heard.

Baum is a small and inconsequential flower blooming in the shade of Shakespeare. I suppose I will be reviled for mentioning them in one paragraph. But both lived inside their heads with a mind gone wild with wanting, wishing, hoping, shaping, dreaming. There, if no other place, they touch fingertips.

In a world where books are machine-made for "age groups" and pass through dry-parchment analysts' hands before being pill-fed to kids, Baum deserves this book, because Baum is needed. When the cities die, in their present form at least, and we head out into Eden again, which we must and will, Baum will be waiting for us. And if the road we take is not Yellow Brick why, damn it, we can imagine that it is, even as we imagine our wives beautiful and our husbands wise and our children kind until such day as they echo that dream. . . .

In this William Stout story sketch, a talking owl greets visitors "Entering The Forest" at the proposed "Cowardly Lion's Haunted Forest" dark ride for the *Wonderful World of Oz*-themed Entertainment Resort.

ON REREADING THE OZ BOOKS

by Gore Vidal

In the preface to *The Wizard of Oz*, L. Frank Baum says that he would like to create *modern* fairy tales by departing from Grimm and Andersen and "all the horrible and blood-curdling incident devised" by such authors "to point a fearsome moral." Baum then makes the disingenuous point that "Modern education includes morality; therefore the modern child seeks only entertainment in its wonder-tales and gladly dispenses with all disagreeable incident." Yet there is a certain amount of explicit as well as implicit moralizing in the Oz books; there are also "disagreeable incidents," and people do, somehow, die even though death and illness are not supposed to exist in Oz.

I have reread the Oz books in the order in which they were written. Some things are as I remember. Others strike me as being entirely new. I was struck by the unevenness of style not only from book to book but, sometimes, from page to page. The jaggedness can be explained by the fact that the man who was writing fourteen Oz books was writing forty-eight other books at the same time. Arguably, *The Wizard of Oz* is the best of the lot. After all, the first book is the one in which Oz was invented. Yet, as a child, I preferred *The Emerald City, Rinkitink*, and *The Lost Princess* to *The Wizard*. Now I find that all of the books tend to flow together in a single narrative, with occasional bad patches.

In *The Wizard of Oz* Dorothy is about six years old. In the later books she seems to be ten or eleven. Baum locates her swiftly and efficiently in the first sentence of the series. "Dorothy lived in the midst of the great Kansas prairies, with Uncle Henry, who was a farmer, and Aunt Em, who was the farmer's wife." The landscape would have confirmed John Ruskin's dark view of American scenery (he died the year that *The Wizard of Oz* was published).

> When Dorothy stood in the doorway and looked around, she could see nothing but the great gray prairie on every side. Not a tree nor a house broke the broad sweep of flat country that reached the edge of the sky in all directions.

This is the plain American style at its best. Like most of Baum's central characters Dorothy lacks the regulation father and mother. Some commentators have made, I think, too much of Baum's parentless children. The author's motive seems to me to be not only obvious but sensible. A child separated from loving parents for any length of time is going to be distressed, even in a magic story. But aunts and uncles need not be taken too seriously.

In the first four pages Baum demonstrates the drabness of Dorothy's life, the next two pages are devoted to the cyclone that lifts the house into the air and hurls it to Oz. Newspaper accounts of recent cyclones had obviously impressed Baum. Alone in the house (except for Toto, a Cairn terrier), Dorothy is established as a sensible girl who is not going to worry unduly about events that she cannot control. The house crosses the Deadly Desert and lands on top of the Wicked Witch of the West who promptly dries up and dies. Right off, Baum breaks his own rule that no one ever dies in Oz. I used to spend a good deal of time worrying about the numerous inconsistencies in the sacred texts. From time to time, Baum himself would try to rationalize errors but he was far too quick and careless a writer ever to create the absolutely logical mad worlds that Lewis Carroll or E. Nesbit did.

Dorothy is acclaimed by the Munchkins as a good witch who has managed to free them from the Wicked Witch. They advise her to go to the Emerald City and try to see the famous Wizard; he alone would have the power to grant her dearest wish, which is to go home to Kansas. Why she wanted to go back was never clear to me. Or, finally, to Baum: eventually, he moves Dorothy (with aunt and uncle) to Oz.

Along the way to the Emerald City, Dorothy meets a live Scarecrow in search of brains, a Tin Woodman in search of a heart, a Cowardly Lion in search of courage. Each new character furthers the plot. Each is essentially a humor. Each, when he speaks, strikes the same simple, satisfying note.

Together they undergo adventures. In sharp contrast to gray flat Kansas, Oz seems to blaze with color. Yet the Emerald City is a bit of a fraud. Everyone is obliged to wear green glasses in order to make the city appear emerald-green.

The Wizard says that he will help them if they destroy yet another wicked witch. They do. Only to find out that the Wizard is a fake who arrived by balloon from the States, where he had been a magician in a circus. Although a fraud, the Wizard is a good psychologist. He gives the Scarecrow bran for brains, the Tin Woodman a red velvet heart, the Cowardly Lion a special courage syrup. Each has now become what he wanted to be (and was all along). The Wizard's response to their delight is glum: " 'How can I help being a humbug,' he said, 'when all these people make me do things that everybody knows can't be done? It was easy to make the Scarecrow and the Lion and the Woodman happy, because they imagined I could do anything. But it will take more than imagination to carry Dorothy back to Kansas, and I'm sure I don't know how it can be done.' " When the Wizard arranges a balloon to take Dorothy and himself back home, the balloon takes off without Dorothy. Finally, she is sent home through the intervention of magic, and the good witch Glinda.

The style of the first book is straightforward, even formal. There are almost no contractions. Dorothy speaks not at all the way a grownup might think a child should speak but like a sensible somewhat literal person. There are occasional Germanisms (did Baum's father speak German?): "'What is that little animal you are so tender of?'" Throughout all the books there is a fascination with jewelry and elaborate costumes. Baum never got over his love of theater. In this he resembled his favorite author Charles Reade, of whom *The Dictionary of National Biography* tells us: "At his best Reade was an admirable storyteller, full of resource and capacity to excite terror and pity, but his ambition to excel as a dramatist militated against his success as a novelist, and nearly all his work is disfigured by a striving after theatrical effect."

Baum's passion for the theater and, later, the movies not only wasted his time but, worse, it had a noticeably bad effect on his prose style. Because *The Wizard of Oz* was the most successful children's book of the 1900 Christmas season..., Baum was immediately inspired to dramatize the story. Much "improved" by other hands, the musical comedy opened in Chicago (June 16, 1902) and was a success. After a year and a half on Broadway, the show toured off and on until 1911. Over the years Baum was to spend a good deal of time trying to make plays and films based on the Oz characters. Except for the first, none was a success.

Since two popular vaudevillians had made quite a splash as the Tin Woodman and the Scarecrow in the musical version of the *Wizard*, Baum decided that a sequel was in order... for the stage. But rather than write directly for the theater, he chose to write a second Oz book, without

Dorothy or the Wizard. In an Author's Note to *The Marvelous Land of Oz*, Baum somewhat craftily says that he has been getting all sorts of letters from children asking him "to 'write something more' about the Scarecrow and the Tin Woodman." In 1904 the sequel was published, with a dedication to the two vaudevillians. A subsequent musical comedy called *The Woggle-Bug* was then produced; and failed. That, for the time being, was that. But the idiocies of popular theater had begun to infect Baum's prose. *The Wizard of Oz* is chastely written. *The Land of Oz* is not. Baum riots in dull word play. There are endless bad puns, of the sort favored by popular comedians. There is also that true period horror: the baby-talking ingenue, a character who lasted well into our day in the menacing shapes of Fanny (Baby Snooks) Brice and the early Ginger Rogers. Dorothy, who talked plainly and to the point in *The Wizard*, talks (when she reappears in the third book) with a cuteness hard to bear. Fortunately, Baum's show-biz phase wore off and in later volumes Dorothy's speech improves.

Despite stylistic lapses, *The Land of Oz* is one of the most unusual and interesting books of the series. In fact, it is so unusual that after the Shirley Temple television adaptation of the book in 1960,* PTA circles were in a state of crisis. The problem that knitted then and, I am told, knits even today many a maternal brow is Sexual Role. Sexual Role makes the world go round. It is what makes the man go

---

*In 1939, MGM made a film called *The Wizard of Oz* with Judy Garland. A new book, *The Making of The Wizard of Oz* by Aljean Hannetz, describes in altogether too great but fascinating detail the assembling of the movie, which had one had a half producers, ten writers, and four directors. Who then was the "auteur"?

to the office or to the factory where he works hard while the wife fulfills *her* Sexual Role by homemaking and consuming and bringing up boys to be real boys and girls to be real girls, a cycle that must continue unchanged and unquestioned until the last car comes off Detroit's last assembly line and the last all-American sun vanishes behind a terminal dioxin haze.

Certainly the denouement of *The Land of Oz* is troubling for those who have heard of Freud. A boy, Tip, is held in thrall by a wicked witch named Mombi. One day she gets hold of an elixir that makes the inanimate live. Tip uses this magical powder to bring to life a homemade figure with a jack-o-lantern head. Jack Pumpkinhead, who turns out to be a comic of the Ed Wynn–Simple Simon school: " 'Now that is a very interesting history,' said Jack, well pleased; 'and I understand it perfectly–all but the explanation.' "

Tip and Jack Pumpkinhead escape from Mombi aboard a brought-to-life sawhorse. Then they meet the stars of the show (and a show it is), the Scarecrow and the Tin Woodman. As a central character neither is very effective. In fact, each has a tendency to sententiousness; and there are nowhere near enough jokes. The Scarecrow goes on about his brains; the Tin Woodman about his heart. But then it is the limitation as well as the charm of made-up fairy-tale creatures to embody to the point of absurdity a single quality of humor.

There is one genuinely funny sketch. When the Scarecrow and Jack Pumpkinhead meet, they decide that since each comes from a different country, " 'We must,' " says the Scarecrow, " 'have an interpreter.'

" 'What is an interpreter?' asked Jack.

" 'A person who understands both my language and your own. . . .' " And so on. Well, maybe this is not so funny.

The Scarecrow (who had taken the vanished Wizard's place as ruler of Oz) is overthrown by a "revolting" army of girls (great excuse for a leggy chorus). This long and rather heavy satire on the suffragettes was plainly more suitable for a Broadway show than for a children's story. The girl leader, Jinjur, is an unexpectedly engaging character. She belongs to the Bismarckian *Realpolitik* school. She is accused of treason for having usurped the Scarecrow's throne. " 'The throne belongs to whoever is able to take it,' answered Jinjur as she slowly ate another caramel. 'I have taken it, as you see; so just now I am the Queen, and all who oppose me are guilty of treason . . .' " This is the old children's game I-am-the-King-of-the-castle, a.k.a. human history.

Among the new characters met in this story are the Woggle-Bug, a highly magnified insect who has escaped from a classroom exhibition and (still magnified) ranges about the countryside. A parody of an American academic, he is addicted to horrendous puns on the grounds that " 'a joke derived from a play upon words is considered among educated people to be eminently proper.' " Anna livia plurabelle.

There is a struggle between Jinjur and the legitimate forces of the Scarecrow. The Scarecrow's faction wins and the girls are sent away to be homemakers and consumers. In passing, the Scarecrow observes, " 'I am convinced that the only people worthy of consideration in this world are the unusual ones. For the common folks are like the leaves of a tree, and live and die unnoticed.' " To which the Tin Woodman replies, " 'Spoken like a philosopher!' " To which the current editor Martin Gardner responds, with true democratic wrath, "This despicable view, indeed defended by many philosophers, had earlier been countered by the Tin Woodman," etc. But the view is not at all despicable. For one thing, it would be the normal view of an odd magical creature who cannot die. For another, Baum was simply echoing those neo-Darwinians who dominated most American thinking for at least a century. It testifies to Baum's sweetness of character that unlike most writers of his day he seldom makes fun of the poor or weak or unfortunate. Also, the Scarecrow's "despicable" remarks can be interpreted as meaning that although unorthodox dreamers are despised by the ordinary, their dreams are apt to prevail in the end and become reality.

Glinda the Good Sorceress is a kindly mother figure to the various children who visit or live in Oz, and it is she who often ties up the loose ends when the story bogs down. In *The Land of Oz* Glinda has not a loose end but something on the order of a hangman's rope to knot. Apparently the rightful ruler of Oz is Princess Ozma. As a baby, Ozma was changed by Mombi into the boy Tip. Now Tip must be restored to his true identity. The PTA went, as it were, into plenary session. What effect would a book like this have on a boy's sense of himself as a future man, breadwinner, and father to more of same? Would he want, awful thought, to be a Girl? Even Baum's Tip is alarmed when told who he is. " 'I!' cried Tip, in amazement. 'Why I'm no Princess Ozma— I'm not a girl!' " Glinda tells him that indeed he was—and really is. Tip is understandably grumpy. Finally, he says to Glinda, " 'I might try it for awhile,—just to see how it seems, you know. But if I don't like being a girl you must promise to change me into a boy again.' " Glinda says that this is not in the cards. Glumly, Tip agrees to the restoration. Tip becomes the beautiful Ozma, who hopes that " 'none of you will care less for me than you did before, I'm just the same Tip, you know, only—only—' "

"Only you're different!" said the Pumpkinhead; and everyone thought it was the wisest speech he had ever made.

Essentially, Baum's human protagonists are neither male nor female but children, a separate category in his view if not in that of our latter-day sexists. Baum's use of sex changes was common to the popular theater of his day, which, in turn, derived from the Elizabethan era when boys played girls whom the plot often required to pretend to be boys. In Baum's *The Enchanted Island of Yew* a fairy (female) becomes a knight (male) in order to have adventures. In *The Emerald City* the hideous Phanfasm leader turns himself into a beautiful woman. When *John Dough and the Cherub* (1906) was published, the sex of the five-year-old cherub was never mentioned in the text; the publishers then launched a national ad campaign: "Is the cherub boy or girl? $500 for the best answers." In those innocent times Tip's metamorphosis as Ozma was nothing more than a classic *coup de théâtre* of the sort that even now requires the boy Peter Pan to be played on stage by a mature woman.

Today of course any sort of sexual metamorphosis causes distress. Although Raylyn Moore in her plot *précis* of *The Enchanted Island of Yew* (in her book *Wonderful Wizard, Marvelous Land*) does make one confusing reference to the protagonist as "he (she)," she omits entirely the Tip/Ozma transformation which is the whole point to *The Land of Oz*, while the plot as given by the publisher Reilly & Lee says only that "the book ends with an amazing surprise, and from that moment on Ozma is princess of all Oz." But, surely, for a pre-pube there is not much difference between a boy and a girl protagonist. After all, the central fact of the pre-pube's existence is not being male or female but being a child, much the hardest of all roles to play. During and after puberty, there is a tendency to want a central character like oneself (my favorite Oz book was R. P. Thompson's *Speedy in Oz*, whose eleven- or twelve-year-old hero could have been, I thought, me). Nevertheless, what matters most even to an adolescent is not the gender of the main character who experiences adventures but the adventures themselves, and the magic, and the jokes, and the pictures.

Dorothy is a perfectly acceptable central character for a boy to read about. She asks the right questions. She is not sappy (as Ozma can sometimes be). She is straight to the point and a bit aggressive. Yet the Dorothy who returns to the series in the third book, *Ozma of Oz* (1907), is somewhat different from the original Dorothy. She is older and her conversation is full of cute contractions that must have doubled up audiences in Sioux City but were pretty hard going for at least one child forty years ago.

To get Dorothy back to Oz there is the by now obligatory natural disaster. The book opens with Dorothy and her uncle on board a ship to Australia. During a storm she is swept overboard. Marius Bewley has noted that this opening chapter "is so close to Crane's ('The Open Boat') in theme, imagery and technique that it is difficult to imagine, on comparing the two in detail, that the similanty is wholly, or even largely accidental."

Dorothy is accompanied by a yellow chicken named Bill. As they are now in magic country, the chicken talks. Since the chicken is a hen, Dorothy renames her Billina. The chicken is fussy and self-absorbed; she is also something of an overachiever: " 'How is my grammar?' asked the yellow hen anxiously." Rather better than Dorothy's, whose dialogue is marred by such Baby Snooksisms as " 'zactly," "auto'biles," " 'lieve," " 'splain."

Dorothy and Billina come ashore in Ev, a magic country on the other side of the Deadly Desert that separates Oz from the real world (what separates such magical kingdoms as Ix and Ev from our realer world is never made plain). In any case, the formula has now been established. Cyclone or storm at sea or earthquake ends not in death for child and animal companion but translation into a magic land. Then, one by one, strange new characters join the travelers. In this story the first addition is Tik-Tok, a clockwork robot (sixteen years later the word "robot" was coined). He has run down. They wind him up. Next they meet Princess Langwidere. She is deeply narcissistic, a trait not much admired by Baum (had he been traumatized by all those actresses and actors he had known on tour?). Instead of changing clothes, hair, makeup, the Princess changes heads from her collection. I found the changing of heads fascinating. And puzzling: since the brains in each head varied, would Langwidere still be herself when she put on a new head or would she become someone else? Thus Baum made logicians of his readers.

The Princess is about to add Dorothy's head to her collection when the marines arrive in the form of Ozma and retinue, who have crossed the Deadly Desert on a magic carpet (cheating, I thought at the time; either a desert is impassable or it is not). Dorothy and Ozma meet, and Dorothy, "as soon as she heard the sweet voice of the girlish ruler of Oz knew that she would learn to love her dearly." That sort of thing I tended to skip.

The principal villain of the Oz canon is now encountered: the Nome King (Baum thought the "g" in front of "nome" too difficult for children . . . how did he think they spelled and pronounced "gnaw"?). Roquat of the Rock lived deep beneath the earth, presiding over his legions of hardworking Nomes (first cousins to George Macdonald's goblins). I was always happy when Baum took us below ground, and showed us fantastic caverns strewn with precious stones where scurrying Nomes did their best to please the bad-tempered Roquat, whose " 'laugh,' " one admirer points out, " 'is worse than another man's frown.' " Ozma and company are transformed into bric-a-brac by Roquat's magic. But Dorothy and Billina outwit Roquat (Nomes fear fresh eggs). Ozma and all the other victims of the Nome King are restored to their former selves, and Dorothy is given an opportunity to ham it up.

> "Royal Ozma, and you, Queen of Ev, I welcome you and your people back to the land of the living. Billina has saved you from your troubles, and now we will leave this drea'ful place, and return to Ev as soon as poss'ble."
> While the child spoke they could all see that she wore the magic belt, and a great cheer went up from all her friends. . . .

Baum knew that nothing so pleases a child as a situation where, for once, the child is in the driver's seat and able to dominate adults. Dorothy's will to power is a continuing force in the series and as a type she is still with us in such popular works as *Peanuts*, where she continues her steely progress toward total dominion in the guise of the relentless Lucy.

Back in the Emerald City, Ozma shows Dorothy her magic picture in which she can see what is happening anywhere in the world. If Dorothy ever wants to visit Oz, all she has to do is make a certain signal and Ozma will transport her from Kansas to Oz. Although this simplified transportation considerably, Baum must have known even then that half the charm of the Oz stories was the scary trip of an ordinary American child from USA to Oz. As a result, in

Dorothy and the Wizard in Oz (1908), another natural catastrophe is used to bring Dorothy back to Oz; the long-
missing Wizard, too. Something like the San Francisco
earthquake happens. Accompanied by a dim boy called Zeb
and a dull horse called Jim, Dorothy falls deep into the
earth. This catastrophe really got to Dorothy and "for a few
moments the little girl lost consciousness. Zeb, being a boy,
did not faint, but he was badly frightened. . . ." That is
Baum's one effort to give some sort of points to a boy. He
promptly forgets about Zeb, and Dorothy is back in the sad-
dle, running things. She is aided by the Wizard, who joins
them in his balloon.

Deep beneath the earth are magical countries (inspired
by Verne's *Journey to the Center of the Earth*, 1864? Did
Verne or Baum inspire Burroughs' *Pellucidar*, 1923?). In a
country that contains vegetable people, a positively Golden
Bough note is sounded by the ruling Prince: " 'One of the
most unpleasant things about our vegetable lives [is] that
while we are in our full prime we must give way to another,
and be covered up in the ground to sprout and grow and
give birth to other people.' " But then according to the various biographies, Baum was interested in Hinduism, and the
notion of karma.

After a number of adventures Dorothy gestures to Ozma
(she certainly took her time about it, I thought) and they are
all transported to the Emerald City where the usual party is
given for them, carefully described in a small-town newspaper style of the Social-Notes-from-all-over variety. *The
Road to Oz* (1909) is the mixture as before. In Kansas,
Dorothy meets the Shaggy Man; he is a tramp of the sort

that haunted the American countryside after the Civil War when unemployed veterans and men ruined by the depressions of the 1870s took to the road where they lived and died, no doubt, brutishly. The Shaggy Man asks her for directions. Exasperated by the tramp's slowness to figure out her instructions, she says: " 'You're so stupid. Wait a minute till I run in the house and get my sunbonnet.' " Dorothy is easily "provoked." " 'My, but you're clumsy!' said the little girl." She gives him a "severe look." Then " 'Come on,' she commanded." She then leads him to the wrong, i.e., the magical, road to Oz.

With *The Emerald City of Oz* (1910) Baum is back in form. He has had to face up to the fact that Dorothy's trips from the USA to Oz are getting not only contrived, but pointless. If she likes Oz so much, why doesn't she settle there? But if she does, what will happen to her uncle and aunt? Fortunately, a banker is about to foreclose the mortgage on Uncle Henry's farm. Dorothy will have to go to work, says Aunt Em, stricken. " 'You might do housework for someone, dear, you are so handy; or perhaps you could be a nursemaid to little children.' " Dorothy is having none of this. "Dorothy smiled. 'Wouldn't it be funny,' she said, 'for me to do housework in Kansas, when I'm a Princess in the Land of Oz?' " The old people buy this one with surprisingly little fuss. It is decided that Dorothy will signal Ozma, and depart for the Emerald City.

Although Baum's powers of invention seldom flagged, he had no great skill at plot-making. Solutions to problems are arrived at either through improbable coincidence or by bringing in, literally, some god (usually Glinda) from the machine to set things right. Since the narratives are swift and the conversations sprightly and the invented characters are both homely and amusing (animated paper dolls, jigsaw puzzles, pastry, cutlery, china, etc.), the stories never lack momentum. Yet there was always a certain danger that the narrative would flatten out into a series of predictable turns.

In *The Emerald City,* Baum sets in motion two simultaneous plots. The Nome King Roquat decides to conquer Oz. Counterpoint to his shenanigans are Dorothy's travels through Oz with her uncle and aunt (Ozma has given them asylum). Once again, the child's situation *vis à vis* the adult is reversed.

> "Don't be afraid," she said to them. "You are now in the Land of Oz, where you are to live always, and be comfer'ble an' happy. You'll never have to worry over anything again, 'cause there won't be anything to worry about. And you owe it all to the kindness of my friend Princess Ozma."

And never forget it, one hears her mutter to herself.

But while the innocents are abroad in Oz, dark clouds are gathering. Roquat is on the march. I must say that the Nome King has never been more (to me) attractive as a character than in this book. For one thing, the bad temper is almost permanently out of control. It is even beginning to worry the king himself: " 'To be angry once in a while is really good fun, because it makes others so miserable. But to be angry morning, noon and night, as I am, grows monotonous and prevents my gaining any other pleasure in life.' "

Rejecting the offer of the usual anodyne, a "glass of melted silver," Roquat decides to put together an alliance of all the wicked magic figures in order to conquer Oz. He looks among his nomes for an ideal general. He finds him: "I hate good people . . . That is why I am so fond of your Majesty.' " Later the General enlists new allies with the straightforward pitch: " 'Permit me to call your attention to the exquisite joy of making the happy unhappy,' said he at last. 'Consider the pleasure of destroying innocent and harmless people.' " This argument proves irresistible.

The Nomes and their allies make a tunnel beneath the Deadly Desert (but surely its Deadliness must go deeper than they could burrow?). Ozma watches all of them on her magic picture. She is moderately alarmed. " 'But I do not wish to fight,' declared Ozma, firmly." She takes an extremely high and moral American line; one that Woodrow Wilson echoed a few years later when he declared that the United States "is too proud to fight" powerful Germany (as opposed to weak Mexico where Wilson had swallowed his pride just long enough for us to launch an invasion). " 'Because the Nome King intends to do evil is no excuse for my doing the same.' " Ozma has deep thoughts on the nature of evil; " 'I must not blame King Roquat too severely, for he is a Nome and his nature is not so gentle as my own.' " Luckily, Ozite cunning carries the day.

Baum's nicest conceit in *The Emerald City* is Rigamarole Town. Or, as a local boy puts it,

"if you have traveled very much you will have noticed that every town differs from every other

town in one way or another and so by observing the
methods of the people and the way they live as well
as the style of their dwelling places,"

etc. Dorothy and her party are duly impressed by the boy's
endless commentary. He is matched almost immediately by
a woman who tells them, apropos nothing:

"It is the easiest thing in the world for a person to
say 'yes' or 'no' when a question that is asked for the
purpose of gaining information or satisfying the
curiosity of the one who has given expression to the
inquiry has attracted the attention of an individual
who may be competent either from personal experience or the experience of others,"

etc. A member of Dorothy's party remarks that if those people wrote books "it would take a whole library to say the
cow jumped over the moon.' " So it would. And so it does.
The Shaggy Man decides that there is a lot to be said for the
way that people of Oz encourage these people to live
together in one town "while Uncle Sam lets [them] roam
around wild and free, to torture innocent people.' "
Many enthusiasts of the Oz books (among them Ray
Bradbury and Russel B. Nye) point with democratic pride to
the fact that there is a total absence, according to Mr. Nye,
of any "whisper of class consciousness in Oz (as there is in
Alice's Wonderland)." Yet Martin Gardner has already noted
one example of Baum's "despicable" elitism. Later (*Emerald
City*), Baum appears to back away from the view that some

people are better or more special than others. "It seems unfortunate that strong people are usually so disagreeable and overbearing that no one cares for them. In fact, to be different from your fellow creatures is always a misfortune." But I don't think that Baum believed a word of this. If he did, he would have been not L. Frank Baum, creator of the special and magical world of Oz, but Horatio Alger, celebrator of pluck and luck, thrift and drift, money. The dreamy boy with the bad heart at a hated military school was as conscious as any Herman Hesse youth that he was splendidly different from others, and in *The Lost Princess of Oz* Baum reasserts the Scarecrow's position: " 'To be individual, my friends' " (the Cowardly Lion is holding forth), " 'to be different from others, is the only way to become distinguished from the common herd.' "

Inevitably, Baum moved from Chicago to California. Inevitably, he settled in the village of Hollywood in 1909. Inevitably, he made silent films, based on the Oz books. Not so inevitably, he failed for a number of reasons that he could not have foretold. Nevertheless, he put together a half dozen films that (as far as special effects went) were said to be ahead of their time. By 1913 he had returned, somewhat grimly, to writing Oz books, putting Dorothy firmly on ice until the last book of the series.

The final Oz books are among the most interesting. After a gall bladder operation, Baum took to his bed where the last work was done. Yet Baum's imagination seems to have been more than usually inspired despite physical pain and the darkness at hand. *The Lost Princess of Oz* (1917) is one of the best of the series. The beginning is splendidly straightforward. "There could be no doubt of the fact Princess Ozma, the lovely girl ruler of the Fairyland of Oz, was lost. She had completely disappeared." Glinda's magical paraphernalia had also vanished. The search for Ozma involves most of the Oz principals, including Dorothy. The villain Ugu (who had kidnapped and and transformed Ozma) is a most satisfactory character. "A curious thing about Ugu the Shoemaker was that he didn't suspect, in the least, that he was wicked. He wanted to be powerful and great and he hoped to make himself master of all the Land of Oz, that he might compel everyone in that fairy country to obey him. His ambition blinded him to the rights of others and he imagined anyone else would act just as he did if anyone else happened to be as clever as himself." That just about says it all.

In *The Tin Woodman* (1918) a boy named Woot is curious to know what happened to the girl that the Tin Woodman had intended to marry when he was flesh and blood. (Enchanted by a witch, he kept hacking off his own limbs; replacements in tin were provided by a magical smith. Eventually, he was all tin, and so no longer a suitable husband for a flesh and blood girl; he moved away.) Woot, the Tin Woodman, and the Scarecrow (the last two are rather like an old married couple, chatting in a desultory way about the past) set out to find the girl. To their astonishment, they meet another tin man. He, too, had courted the girl. He, too, had been enchanted by the witch; had chopped himself to bits; had been reconstituted by the same magical smith. The two tin men wonder what has happened to the girl. They also wonder what happened to their original imperishable pieces.

In due course, the Tin Woodman is confronted by his original head. I have never forgotten how amazed I was not only by Baum's startling invention but by the drawing of the Tin Woodman staring into the cupboard where sits his old head. The Tin Woodman is amazed, too. But the original head is simply bored, and snippy. When asked "What relation *are* we?" The head replies, " 'Don't ask me. . . . For my part, I'm not anxious to claim relationship with any common, manufactured article, like you. You may be all right in your class, but your class isn't my class.' " When the Tin Woodman asks the head what it thinks about inside the cupboard, he is told,

> "Nothing. . . . A little reflection will convince you that I have had nothing to think about, except the boards on the inside of the cupboard door, and it didn't take me long to think everything about those boards that could be thought of. Then, of course, I quit thinking."
> "And are you happy?"
> "Happy? What's that?"

There is a further surprise when the Tin Woodman discovers that his old girlfriend has married a creature made up of various human parts assembled from him and from the other man of tin. The result is a most divided and unsatisfactory man, and for the child reader a fascinating problem in the nature of identity.

In Baum's last Oz book, *Glinda of Oz* (posthumously published in 1920), magic is pretty much replaced by complex machinery. There is a doomed island that can sink beneath the waters of a lake at the mention of a secret word, but though the word is magic, the details of how the island rises and sinks are straight out of *Popular Mechanics*.

Ozma and Dorothy are trapped beneath the water of the lake by yet another narcissistic princess, Coo-ee-oh. By the time Glinda comes to the rescue, Coo-ee-oh has been turned into a proud and vapid swan. This book is very much a last round-up. . . . Certainly there are some uncharacteristic sermons in favor of the Protestant work ethic: "Dorothy wished in her kindly, innocent heart, that all men and women could be fairies with silver wands, and satisfy all their needs without so much work and worry. . . ." Ozma fields that one as briskly as the Librarian of Detroit could want:

> "No, no, Dorothy, that wouldn't do at all. Instead of happiness your plan would bring weariness. There would be no eager striving to obtain the difficult. . . . There would be nothing to do, you see, and no interest in life and in our fellow creatures."

But Dorothy is not so easily convinced. She notes that Ozma is a magical creature, and *she* is happy. But only, says Ozma, with grinding sweetness, " 'because I can use my fairy powers to make others happy.' " Then Ozma makes the sensible point that although she has magical powers, others like Glinda have even greater powers than she and so " 'there still are things in both nature and in wit for me to marvel at.' "

In Dorothy's last appearance as heroine, she saves the day. She guesses, correctly, that the magic word is the wicked Coo-ee-oh's name. Incidentally, as far as I know, not a single Oz commentator has noted that Coo-ee-oh is the traditional cry of the hog-caller. The book ends with a stern admonishment, " 'it is always wise to do one's duty, however unpleasant that duty may seem tɔ be.' "

Although it is unlikely that Baum would have found Ruskin's aesthetics of much interest, he might well have liked his political writings, particularly *Munera Pulveris* and *Fors*. Ruskin's protégé William Morris would have approved of Oz, where

> Everyone worked half the time and played half the time, and the people enjoyed the work as much as they did the play. . . . There were no cruel overseers set to watch them, and no one to rebuke them and find fault with them. So each one was proud to do all he could for his friends and neighbors, and was glad when they would accept the things he produced.

Anticipating the wrath of the Librarian of Detroit, who in 1957 found the Oz books to have a "cowardly approach to life," Baum adds, slyly, "I do not suppose such an arrangement would be practical with us." Yet Baum has done no more than to revive in his own terms the original Arcadian dream of America. Or, as Marius Bewley noted, "the tension between technology and pastoralism is one of the things that the Oz books are about, whether Baum was aware of it or not." I think that Baum was very much aware of this tension. In Oz he presents the pastoral dream of Jefferson (the slaves have been replaced by magic and goodwill), and into this Eden he introduces forbidden knowledge in the form of black magic (the machine) which good magic (the values of the pastoral society) must overwhelm.

It is Bewley's view that because "the Ozites are much aware of the scientific nature of magic," Ozma wisely limited the practice of magic. As a result, controlled magic enhances the society just as controlled industrialization could enhance (and perhaps even salvage) a society like ours. Unfortunately, the Nome King has governed the United States for more than a century; and he shows no sign of wanting to abdicate. Meanwhile, the life of the many is definitely nome-ish and the environment has been, perhaps, irreparably damaged. To the extent that Baum makes his readers aware that our country's "practical" arrangements are inferior to those of Oz, he is a truly subversive writer and it is no wonder that the Librarian of Detroit finds him cowardly and negative, because, of course, he is brave and affirmative. But then the United States has always been a Rigamarole land where adjectives tend to mean their opposite, when they mean at all.

Despite the Librarian of Detroit's efforts to suppress magical alternative worlds, the Oz books continue to exert their spell. "You do not educate a man by telling him what he knew not," wrote John Ruskin, "but by making him what he was not." In Ruskin's high sense, Baum was a true educator, and those who read his Oz books are often made what they were not—imaginative, tolerant, alert to wonders, life.

This "Cowardly Lion" illustration reflects the influences of Arthur Rackham and John R. Neill on William Stout's work.

A bust of Dorothy awaits visitors just within the doorway of William Stout's "Munchkin Hall of Fame" design for the proposed *Wonderful World of Oz*-themed Entertainment Resort.

FLIMFLAM LAND

Long before Harry Potter,
another wizard held thrall
by Nicholas von Hoffman

On August 1, 1900, a clerk in the Librarian of Congress's copyright office opened a letter that read, "Enclosed please find check for $2.20 for which please enter for copyright and send certificates of same of the two following books." The first of the two was the long-since-forgotten *The Navy Alphabet*, by L Frank Baum, in whose hand the letter was written. The second was *The Wonderful Wizard of Oz*.

A little more than a month later, on September 8, 1900, the now copyrighted *Wizard* was the subject of an enthusiastic piece in *The New York Times Saturday Review of Books and Art*. "The book has a bright and joyous atmosphere, and does not dwell upon killing and deeds of violence," the unsigned article concluded. "Enough stirring adventure enters into it, however, to flavor it with zest, and it will indeed be strange if there be a normal child who will not enjoy the story."

Thus was the Wizard given to the world. Now, a century later, Dorothy, Toto, and all the gang are back at the Library of Congress, which is throwing them a birthday party of sorts, by means of an exhibition (the last of four marking the Library's two centuries of existence). Opening on April 22, the show will contain a wide variety of books, artifacts, illustrations, motion pictures, recordings, and commercial gimcracks related to the land of Oz—not to mention the Cowardly Lion's wig and, possibly, a pair of Dorothy's ruby shoes from the 1939 Judy Garland movie. This last item will cause a mild case of hives in true *amateurs d'Oz*; as they often remind people, in the book the slippers were silver.

Some Oz lovers may find this homage to Baum quite out of character for a library; many of them believe that librarians have long taken a dim view of Dorothy and her friends. Indeed, the books were difficult to find in libraries during the first part of this century. Some librarians seemed to find them silly and insubstantial, while others took issue with their tales of witchcraft—shades of the Harry Potter controversy. Even today, say Oz scholars, libraries often choose not to stock the books. (Not so the Library of Congress, whose collection includes copies in Spanish, Russian, German, Romanian, Latin, Hebrew, and Arabic.)

In the 1950s, Gore Vidal wrote an essay for the *New York Review of Books* that revealed him to be an unreconstructed Oz-ophile; on the question of librarian antipathy to the Wizard, he noted that librarians "have made the practical point that if you buy one volume of a popular series you will have to get the whole lot and there are, after all, 40 Oz books." Only 14 were written by Baum, although the books in the series written by Ruth Plumly Thompson meet with the approval of many Ozmatics, including Vidal, who said the books were a major element in his growing up. "Like most Americans my age (with access to books) I spent a good deal of my youth in Baum's Land of Oz," he wrote. "I have a precise, tactile memory of the first Oz book that came into my hands. It was the original 1910 edition of *The Emerald City of Oz*. I still remember the look and the feel of those dark blue covers, the evocative smell of dust and old ink. I also remember that I could not stop reading and rereading the book. But 'reading' is not the right word. In some mysterious way, I was translating myself to Oz, a place which I was to inhabit for many years. . . .With *The Emerald City*, I became addicted to reading."

Vidal is by no means alone in his special nostalgia for an Oz-filled childhood. Michele Slung, the anthologist and literary critic, has similarly happy recollections. "I first began to get the Oz books when I was about nine or ten in Louisville, Kentucky, where I was born and grew up," she says. "I believe they are what helped me stop biting my fingernails. For every fingernail that I successfully grew, I would get a new Oz book. . . . By the time I was a grown-up, I think I had all but three or four."

Without taking up the cudgels for librarians who have disparaged the stories, I—an adult lately come to Oz—do sense something comic-booky about the books' characters. They remind me, if only slightly, of the inane action heroes today's children are taught by the fast-food chains to venerate. I can see how some librarians of the past might find the constructions of the Baum imagination to be somewhat down-market.

Maybe this impression arises from comparing Dorothy of Kansas and Oz with Alice of England and Wonderland. "*Alice* is cerebral. *Oz* is visceral," Slung has written. "Wordplay, political satire, picaresque structure—these are a few of the . . . elements *Oz* and *Wonderland* share. Where they differ has to do with the background and milieu of their authors. Yet, little Anglophile that I was, I never wanted to visit down-the-rabbit-hole or meet any of Carroll's characters. The lilt and the language and the nonsense, plus the innate snobbery, were enough to intrigue me, but at a distance. Oz, on the other hand, was a place I've never stopped wanting to be."

The various supporters of Dorothy and Alice may be like the people who prefer Dickens to Thackeray or vice versa: The two writers may be only just similar enough so that those who like one are probably going to find the other boring or repellent. Dickens and Thackeray, however, were both of the same nationality; Carroll and Baum were not, and their respective fantasy lands reflect this fact. Frank J. Evina, the Library's resident Oz-ologist and the specialist who is curating the exhibit, calls Oz "an American icon" and says that Baum is "America's Hans Christian Andersen. Really, there is no doubt about it."

Although Baum maintained that *Oz* was a fairy tale written for modern kids, some have seen deeper meanings in it. The spring 1964 volume of *American Quarterly* carried an article by Henry M. Littlefield entitled "The Wizard of Oz: Parable on Populism." As Littlefield would have it, the yellow brick road is the gold standard; Dorothy's silver slippers are free coinage of the selfsame precious metal; the Cowardly Lion represents William Jennings Bryan; and the Wizard himself stands for "everyman" presidents such as Benjamin Harrison. This invisible-ink interpretation is clever and endures to this day, although students of Oz, to a man and to a woman, dismiss it—pointing out that Baum seems to have had very little interest in politics, despite having lived through the politically tumultuous 1890s.

Baum, says Evina, "wrote a classic tale, which has had an incredible effect on the American psyche. I just went to the credit union, and they're advertising a loan special using the ruby slippers and the yellow brick road. It's just amazing, no matter where you turn." Of course, some credit for the tale's endurance must also go to the minds behind the 1939 movie adaptation. Were it not for Judy Garland and Metro-Goldwyn-Maver, many of us would know about Kansas and its cyclones, but not about Toto and the Tin Man.

Still, many Oz fanciers believe it is the story's distinctly American character that has won it a place in the national consciousness. Baum's world is a peculiarly American fairyland, characterized not by enigmatic magic but by the products of a tinker's or inventor's imagination. Oz is a mechanic's fantasy in which the workings of the miraculous are often revealed and explained—as exemplified in the Wizard's showing Dorothy and her friends exactly how he was able to flimflam the local witches and pull off his humbug. When the gang discovers that the Wizard is not a terrifying disembodied head, but a harmless con man, Baum shows the reader how the trick was done:

> He led the way to a small chamber in the rear of the Throne Room, and they all followed him. He pointed to one corner, in which lay the Great Head, made out of many thicknesses of paper, and with a carefully painted face. "This I hung from the ceiling by a wire," said Oz. "I stood behind the screen and pulled a thread, to make the eyes move and the mouth open."

In such scenes one can imagine the Wizard as a stand-in for the author himself, whom Slung calls "one of those great American types who just kept inventing himself and having entrepreneurial ideas."

Born in upstate New York in 1856, Frank Baum was one of the many wandering Americans of his generation. The late 1880s found him in Aberdeen, South Dakota, first opening a department store and then working on a newspaper. A few years later he popped up in Chicago; he eventually settled in California. Along the way, Baum failed in the axle-grease business, managed an opera house and a baseball team, and was a traveling salesman and buyer for a department store before becoming the editor of *The Show Window* for the National Association of Window Trimmers. What could be more American in its way than a periodical teaching small retailers how to decorate their shop windows?

If he was typically American, there also is a sweetly daft quality to Baum's adventures. One might think of him as an Oz-American. When he moved to Pasadena, he erected in his garden a huge birdcage stocked with songbirds where— evidently oblivious to the potential of overhead bombard- ment—he wrote his books.

His output was prodigious. He covered topics both fan- tastical and practical, such as *The Book of the Hamburgs, A Brief Treatise Upon the Mating, Rearing, and Management of the Different Varieties of Hamburgs.* (For you city people who think eggs come from the supermarket: Hamburgs are a flashy looking variety of chicken with a reputation for producing eggs with satisfying regularity.) Baum's pen also scratched out children's stories, articles, plays, musicals, and adult novels published under his own name as well as an impressive variety of noms de plume: Louis F. Baum, Schuyler Staunton, Floyd Akers, Laura Bancroft, John Estes Cooke, Captain Hugh Fitzgerald, Suzanne Metcalf, and Edith Van Dyne, the name he used for the highly successful *Aunt Jane's Nieces* series.

All this work paled in comparison to *The Wonderful Wizard of Oz*, however, and most of it is long forgotten. The story was so popular from the first that Frank Baum was never able to elude his own success. Not that he tried too hard, when the nation's children were imploring him for more and more Oz.

After the publication of his first children's book, *Mother Goose in Prose*, the 39-year-old author inscribed a copy to his sister; it may well reveal the true disposition of Lyman Frank Baum's heart. "My dear Mary," the inscription reads.

"When I was young I longed to write a great novel that should win me fame. Now that I am getting old my first book is written to amuse children. For, aside from my evident inability to do anything 'great,' I have learned to regard fame as a will-o-the-wisp, which, when caught, is not worth the possession; but to please a child is a sweet and lovely thing that warms one's heart and brings its own reward."

In this William Stout watercolor, the Wicked Witch of the West transforms herself into a green, fire-breathing "Witch Dragon" inside a dark ride at the proposed *Wonderful World of Oz*-themed Entertainment Resort.

INTRODUCTION

by L. Frank Baum

Folk lore, legends, myths and fairy tales have followed childhood through the ages, for every healthy youngster has a wholesome and instinctive love for stories fantastic, marvelous and manifestly unreal. The winged fairies of Grimm and Andersen have brought more happiness to childish hearts than all other human creations.

Yet the old-time fairy tale, having served for generations, may now be classed as "historical" in the children's library; for the time has come for a series of newer "wonder tales" in which the stereotyped genie, dwarf and fairy are eliminated, together with all the horrible and bloodcurdling incident devised by their authors to point a fearsome moral to each tale. Modern education includes morality; therefore the modern child seeks only entertainment in its wonder-tales and gladly dispenses with all disagreeable incident.

Having this thought in mind, the story of *The Wonderful Wizard of Oz* was written solely to pleasure children of today. It aspires to being a modernized fairy tale, in which the wonderment and joy are retained and the heart-aches and nightmares are left out.

L. Frank Baum

Chicago,

April, 1900

LIST OF CHAPTERS

This book is dedicated to my
good friend & comrade.
My wife
L.F.B.

" She caught Toto by the ear."

CHAPTER I

THE CYCLONE

DOROTHY LIVED in the midst of the great Kansas prairies, with Uncle Henry, who was a farmer, and Aunt Em, who was the farmer's wife. Their house was small, for the lumber to build it had to be carried by wagon many miles. There were four walls, a floor and a roof, which made one room; and this room contained a rusty looking cooking stove, a cupboard for the dishes, a table, three or four chairs, and the beds. Uncle Henry and Aunt Em had a big bed in one corner, and Dorothy a little bed in another corner. There was no garret at all, and no cellar—except a small hole, dug in the ground, called a cyclone cellar, where the family could go in case one of those great whirlwinds arose, mighty enough to crush any building in its path. It was reached by a trap-door in the middle of the floor, from which a ladder led down into the small, dark hole.

When Dorothy stood in the doorway and looked around, she could see nothing but the great gray prairie on every side. Not a tree nor a house broke the broad sweep of flat country that reached the edge of the sky in all directions. The sun had baked the plowed land into a gray mass, with little cracks running through it. Even the grass was not green, for the sun had burned the tops of the long blades until they were the same gray color to be seen everywhere. Once the house had been painted, but the sun blistered the paint and the rains washed it away, and now the house was as dull and gray as everything else.

When Aunt Em came there to live she was a young, pretty wife. The sun and wind had changed her, too. They had taken the sparkle from her eyes and left them a sober gray; they had taken the red from her cheeks and lips, and they were gray also. She was thin and gaunt, and never smiled, now. When Dorothy, who was an orphan, first came to her, Aunt Em had been so startled by the child's laughter that she would scream and press her hand upon her heart whenever Dorothy's merry voice reached her ears; and she still looked at the little girl with wonder that she could find anything to laugh at.

Uncle Henry never laughed. He worked hard from morning till night and did not know what joy was. He was gray also, from his long beard to his rough boots, and he looked stern and solemn, and rarely spoke.

It was Toto that made Dorothy laugh, and saved her from growing as gray as her other surroundings. Toto was not gray; he was a little black dog, with long, silky hair and small black eyes that twinkled merrily on either side of his funny, wee nose. Toto played all day long, and Dorothy played with him, and loved him dearly.

To-day, however, they were not playing. Uncle Henry sat upon the door-step and looked anxiously at the sky, which was even grayer than usual. Dorothy stood in the door with Toto in her arms, and looked at the sky too. Aunt Em was washing the dishes.

From the far north they heard a low wail of the wind, and Uncle Henry and Dorothy could see where the long grass bowed in waves before the coming storm. There now came a sharp whistling in the air from the south, and as they turned their eyes that way they saw ripples in the grass coming from that direction also.

Suddenly Uncle Henry stood up.

"There's a cyclone coming, Em," he called to his wife; "I'll go look after the stock." Then he ran toward the sheds where the cows and horses were kept.

Aunt Em dropped her work and came to the door. One glance told her of the danger close at hand.

"Quick, Dorothy!" she screamed; "run for the cellar!"

Toto jumped out of Dorothy's arms and hid under the bed, and the girl started to get him. Aunt Em, badly frightened, threw open the trap-door in the floor and climbed down the ladder into the small, dark hole. Dorothy caught Toto at last, and started to follow her aunt. When she was half way across the room there came a great shriek from the wind, and the house shook so hard that she lost her footing and sat down suddenly upon the floor.

A strange thing then happened.

The house whirled around two or three times and rose slowly through the air. Dorothy felt as if she were going up in a balloon.

The north and south winds met where the house stood, and made it the exact center of the cyclone. In the middle of a cyclone the air is generally still, but the great pressure of the wind on every side of the house raised it up higher and higher, until it was at the very top of the cyclone; and there it remained and was carried miles and miles away as easily as you could carry a feather.

It was very dark, and the wind howled horribly around her, but Dorothy found she was riding quite easily. After the first few whirls around, and one other time when the house tipped badly, she felt as if she were being rocked gently, like a baby in a cradle.

Toto did not like it. He ran about the room, now here, now there, barking loudly; but Dorothy sat quite still on the floor and waited to see what would happen.

Once Toto got too near the open trap-door, and fell in; and at first the little girl thought she had lost him. But soon she saw one of his ears sticking up through the hole, for the strong pressure of the air was keeping him up so that he could not fall. She crept to the hole, caught Toto by the ear, and dragged him into the room again; afterward closing the trap-door so that no more accidents could happen.

Hour after hour passed away, and slowly Dorothy got over her fright; but she felt quite lonely, and the wind shrieked so loudly all about her that she nearly became deaf. At first she had wondered if she would be dashed to pieces when the house fell again; but as the hours passed and nothing terrible happened, she stopped worrying and resolved to wait calmly and see what the future would bring. At last she crawled over the swaying floor to her bed, and lay down upon it; and Toto followed and lay down beside her.

In spite of the swaying of the house and the wailing of the wind, Dorothy soon closed her eyes and fell fast asleep.

" I am the Witch of the North."

CHAPTER II

THE COUNCIL WITH THE MUNCHKINS

S HE WAS awakened by a shock, so sudden and severe that if Dorothy had not been lying on the soft bed she might have been hurt. As it was, the jar made her catch her breath and wonder what had happened; and Toto put his cold little nose into her face and whined dismally. Dorothy sat up and noticed that the house was not moving; nor was it dark, for the bright sunshine came in at the window, flooding the little room. She sprang from her bed and with Toto at her heels ran and opened the door.

The little girl gave a cry of amazement and looked about her, her eyes growing bigger and bigger at the wonderful sights she saw.

The cyclone had set the house down, very gently—for a cyclone—in the midst of a country of marvelous beauty.

There were lovely patches of green sward all about, with stately trees bearing rich and luscious fruits. Banks of gorgeous flowers were on every hand, and birds with rare and brilliant plumage sang and fluttered in the trees and bushes. A little way off was a small brook, rushing and sparkling along between green banks, and murmuring in a voice very grateful to a little girl who had lived so long on the dry, gray prairies.

While she stood looking eagerly at the strange and beautiful sights, she noticed coming toward her a group of the queerest people she had ever seen. They were not as big as the grown folk she had always been used to; but neither were they very small. In fact, they seemed about as tall as Dorothy, who was a well-grown child for her age, although they were, so far as looks go, many years older.

Three were men and one a woman, and all were oddly dressed. They wore round hats that rose to a small point a foot above their heads, with little bells around the brims that tinkled sweetly as they moved. The hats of the men were blue; the little woman's hat was white, and she wore a white gown that hung in plaits from her shoulders; over it were sprinkled little stars that glistened in the sun like diamonds. The men were dressed in blue, of the same shade as their hats, and wore well polished boots with a deep roll of blue at the tops. The men, Dorothy thought, were about as old as Uncle Henry, for two of them had beards. But the little woman was doubtless much older: her face was covered with wrinkles, her hair was nearly white, and she walked rather stiffly.

When these people drew near the house where Dorothy was standing in the doorway, they paused and whispered among themselves, as if afraid to come farther. But the little old woman walked up to Dorothy, made a low bow and said, in a sweet voice,

"You are welcome, most noble Sorceress, to the land of the Munchkins. We are so grateful to you for having killed the wicked Witch of the East, and for setting our people free from bondage."

Dorothy listened to this speech with wonder. What could the little woman possibly mean by calling her a sorceress, and saying she had killed the wicked Witch of the East? Dorothy was an innocent, harmless little girl, who had been carried by a cyclone many miles from home; and she had never killed anything in all her life.

But the little woman evidently expected her to answer; so Dorothy said, with hesitation,

"You are very kind; but there must be some mistake. I have not killed anything."

"Your house did, anyway," replied the little old woman, with a laugh; "and that is the same thing. See!" she continued, pointing to the corner of the house; "there are her two toes, still sticking out from under a block of wood."

Dorothy looked, and gave a little cry of fright. There, indeed, just under the corner of the great beam the house rested on, two feet were sticking out, shod in silver shoes with pointed toes.

"Oh, dear! oh, dear!" cried Dorothy, clasping her hands together in dismay; "the house must have fallen on her. What ever shall we do?"

"There is nothing to be done," said the little woman, calmly.

"But who was she?" asked Dorothy.

"She was the wicked Witch of the East, as I said," answered the little woman. "She has held all the Munchkins in bondage for many years, making them slave for her night and day. Now they are all set free, and are grateful to you for the favour."

"Who are the Munchkins?" enquired Dorothy.

"They are the people who live in this land of the East, where the wicked Witch ruled."

"Are you a Munchkin?" asked Dorothy.

"No; but I am their friend, although I live in the land of the North. When they saw the Witch of the East was dead the Munchkins sent a swift messenger to me, and I came at once. I am the Witch of the North."

"Oh, gracious!" cried Dorothy; "are you a real witch?"

"Yes, indeed;" answered the little woman. "But I am a good witch, and the people love me. I am not as powerful as the wicked Witch was who ruled here, or I should have set the people free myself."

"But I thought all witches were wicked," said the girl, who was half frightened at facing a real witch.

"Oh, no; that is a great mistake. There were only four witches in all the Land of Oz, and two of them, those who live in the North and the South, are good witches. I know this is true, for I am one of them myself, and cannot be mistaken. Those who dwelt in the East and the West were, indeed, wicked witches; but now that you have killed one of them, there is but one wicked Witch in all the Land of Oz— the one who lives in the West."

"But," said Dorothy, after a moment's thought, "Aunt

Em has told me that the witches were all dead—years and years ago."

"Who is Aunt Em?" inquired the little old woman.

"She is my aunt who lives in Kansas, where I came from."

The Witch of the North seemed to think for a time, with her head bowed and her eyes upon the ground. Then she looked up and said,

"I do not know where Kansas is, for I have never heard that country mentioned before. But tell me, is it a civilized country?"

"Oh, yes;" replied Dorothy.

"Then that accounts for it. In the civilized countries I believe there are no witches left; nor wizards, nor sorceresses, nor magicians. But, you see, the Land of Oz has never been civilized, for we are cut off from all the rest of the world. Therefore we still have witches and wizards amongst us."

"Who are the Wizards?" asked Dorothy.

"Oz himself is the Great Wizard," answered the Witch, sinking her voice to a whisper. "He is more powerful than all the rest of us together. He lives in the City of Emeralds."

Dorothy was going to ask another question, but just then the Munchkins, who had been standing silently by, gave a loud shout and pointed to the corner of the house where the Wicked Witch had been lying.

"What is it?" asked the little old woman; and looked, and began to laugh. The feet of the dead Witch had disappeared entirely and nothing was left but the silver shoes.

"She was so old," explained the Witch of the North,

"that she dried up quickly in the sun. That is the end of her. But the silver shoes are yours, and you shall have them to wear." She reached down and picked up the shoes, and after shaking the dust out of them handed them to Dorothy.

"The Witch of the East was proud of those silver shoes," said one of the Munchkins; "and there is some charm connected with them; but what it is we never knew."

Dorothy carried the shoes into the house and placed them on the table. Then she came out again to the Munchkins and said,

"I am anxious to get back to my Aunt and Uncle, for I am sure they will worry about me. Can you help me find my way?"

The Munchkins and the Witch first looked at one another, and then at Dorothy, and then shook their heads.

"At the East, not far from here," said one, "there is a great desert, and none could live to cross it."

"It is the same at the South," said another, "for I have been there and seen it. The South is the country of the Quadlings."

"I am told," said the third man, "that it is the same at the West. And that country, where the Winkies live, is ruled by the wicked Witch of the West, who would make you her slave if you passed her way."

"The North is my home," said the old lady, "and at its edge is the same great desert that surrounds this land of Oz. I'm afraid, my dear, you will have to live with us."

Dorothy began to sob, at this, for she felt lonely among all these strange people. Her tears seemed to grieve the kind-hearted Munchkins, for they immediately took out their handkerchiefs and began to weep also. As for the little old woman, she took off her cap and balanced the point on the end of her nose, while she counted "one, two, three" in a solemn voice. At once the cap changed to a slate, on which was written in big, white chalk marks:

"LET DOROTHY GO TO THE CITY OF EMERALDS."

The little old woman took the slate from her nose, and, having read the words on it, asked,

"Is your name Dorothy, my dear?"

"Yes," answered the child, looking up and drying her tears.

"Then you must go to the City of Emeralds. Perhaps Oz will help you."

"Where is this City?" asked Dorothy.

"It is exactly in the center of the country, and is ruled by Oz, the Great Wizard I told you of."

"Is he a good man?" enquired the girl, anxiously.

"He is a good Wizard. Whether he is a man or not I cannot tell, for I have never seen him."

"How can I get there?" asked Dorothy.

"You must walk. It is a long journey, through a country that is sometimes pleasant and sometimes dark and terrible. However, I will use all the magic arts I know of to keep you from harm."

"Won't you go with me?" pleaded the girl, who had begun to look upon the little old woman as her only friend.

"No, I cannot do that," she replied; "but I will give you my kiss, and no one will dare injure a person who has been kissed by the Witch of the North."

She came close to Dorothy and kissed her gently on the

forehead. Where her lips touched the girl they left a round, shining mark, as Dorothy found out soon after.

"The road to the City of Emeralds is paved with yellow brick," said the Witch; "so you cannot miss it. When you get to Oz do not be afraid of him, but tell your story and ask him to help you. Good-bye, my dear."

The three Munchkins bowed low to her and wished her a pleasant journey, after which they walked away through the trees. The Witch gave Dorothy a friendly little nod, whirled around on her left heel three times, and straight-way disappeared, much to the surprise of little Toto, who barked after her loudly enough when she had gone, because he had been afraid even to growl while she stood by.

But Dorothy, knowing her to be a witch, had expected her to disappear in just that way, and was not surprised in the least.

" You must be a great sorceress."

"Dorothy gazed thoughtfully at the Scarecrow."

CHAPTER III

HOW DOROTHY SAVED THE SCARECROW

WHEN DOROTHY was left alone she began to feel hungry. So she went to the cupboard and cut herself some bread, which she spread with butter. She gave some to Toto, and taking a pail from the shelf she carried it down to the little brook and filled it with clear, sparkling water. Toto ran over to the trees and began to bark at the birds sitting there. Dorothy went to get him, and saw such delicious fruit hanging from the branches that she gathered some of it, finding it just what she wanted to help out her breakfast.

Then she went back to the house, and having helped herself and Toto to a good drink of the cool, clear water, she set about making ready for the journey to the City of Emeralds.

Dorothy had only one other dress, but that happened to be clean and was hanging on a peg beside her bed. It was gingham, with checks of white and blue; and although the blue was somewhat faded with many washings, it was still a pretty frock. The girl washed herself carefully, dressed herself in the clean gingham, and tied her pink sunbonnet on her head. She took a little basket and filled it with bread from the cupboard, laying a white cloth over the top. Then she looked down at her feet and noticed how old and worn her shoes were.

"They surely will never do for a long journey, Toto," she said. And Toto looked up into her face with his little black eyes and wagged his tail to show he knew what she meant.

At that moment Dorothy saw lying on the table the silver shoes that had belonged to the Witch of the East.

"I wonder if they will fit me," she said to Toto. "They would be just the thing to take a long walk in, for they could not wear out."

She took off her old leather shoes and tried on the silver ones, which fitted her as well as if they had been made for her.

Finally she picked up her basket.

"Come along, Toto," she said, "we will go to the Emerald City and ask the great Oz how to get back to Kansas again."

She closed the door, locked it, and put the key carefully in the pocket of her dress. And so, with Toto trotting along soberly behind her, she started on her journey.

There were several roads near by, but it did not take her long to find the one paved with yellow brick. Within a short time she was walking briskly toward the Emerald City, her silver shoes tinkling merrily on the hard, yellow roadbed.

The sun shone bright and the birds sang sweet and Dorothy did not feel nearly as bad as you might think a little girl would who had been suddenly whisked away from her own country and set down in the midst of a strange land.

She was surprised, as she walked along, to see how pretty the country was about her. There were neat fences at the sides of the road, painted a dainty blue color, and beyond them were fields of grain and vegetables in abundance. Evidently the Munchkins were good farmers and able to raise large crops. Once in a while she would pass a house, and the people came out to look at her and bow low as she went by; for everyone knew she had been the means of destroying the wicked witch and setting them free from bondage. The houses of the Munchkins were odd looking dwellings, for each was round, with a big dome for a roof. All were painted blue, for in this country of the East blue was the favorite color.

Towards evening, when Dorothy was tired with her long walk and began to wonder where she should pass the night, she came to a house rather larger than the rest. On the green lawn before it many men and women were dancing. Five little fiddlers played as loudly as possible and the people were laughing and singing, while a big table near by was loaded with delicious fruits and nuts, pies and cakes, and many other good things to eat.

The people greeted Dorothy kindly, and invited her to supper and to pass the night with them; for this was the home of one of the richest Munchkins in the land, and his friends were gathered with him to celebrate their freedom from the bondage of the wicked witch.

Dorothy ate a hearty supper and was waited upon by the rich Munchkin himself, whose name was Boq. Then she sat down upon a settee and watched the people dance.

When Boq saw her silver shoes he said,

"You must be a great sorceress."

"Why?" asked the girl.

"Because you wear silver shoes and have killed the wicked witch. Besides, you have white in your frock, and only witches and sorceresses wear white."

"My dress is blue and white checked," said Dorothy, smoothing out the wrinkles in it.

"It is kind of you to wear that," said Boq. "Blue is the color of the Munchkins, and white is the witch color; so we know you are a friendly witch."

Dorothy did not know what to say to this, for all the people seemed to think her a witch, and she knew very well she was only an ordinary little girl who had come by the chance of a cyclone into a strange land.

When she had tired watching the dancing, Boq led her into the house, where he gave her a room with a pretty bed in it. The sheets were made of blue cloth, and Dorothy slept soundly in them till morning, with Toto curled up on the blue rug beside her.

She ate a hearty breakfast, and watched a wee Munchkin baby, who played with Toto and pulled his tail and crowed and laughed in a way that greatly amused Dorothy. Toto was a fine curiosity to all the people, for they had never seen a dog before.

"How far is it to the Emerald City?" the girl asked.

"I do not know," answered Boq, gravely, "for I have

never been there. It is better for people to keep away from Oz, unless they have business with him. But it is a long way to the Emerald City, and it will take you many days. The country here is rich and pleasant, but you must pass through rough and dangerous places before you reach the end of your journey."

This worried Dorothy a little, but she knew that only the great Oz could help her get to Kansas again, so she bravely resolved not to turn back.

She bade her friends good-bye, and again started along the road of yellow brick. When she had gone several miles she thought she would stop to rest, and so climbed to the top of the fence beside the road and sat down. There was a great cornfield beyond the fence, and not far away she saw a Scarecrow, placed high on a pole to keep the birds from the ripe corn.

Dorothy leaned her chin upon her hand and gazed thoughtfully at the Scarecrow. Its head was a small sack stuffed with straw, with eyes, nose and mouth painted on it to represent a face. An old, pointed blue hat, that had belonged to some Munchkin, was perched on this head, and the rest of the figure was a blue suit of clothes, worn and faded, which had also been stuffed with straw. On the feet were some old boots with blue tops, such as every man wore in this country, and the figure was raised above the stalks of corn by means of the pole stuck up its back.

While Dorothy was looking earnestly into the queer, painted face of the Scarecrow, she was surprised to see one of the eyes slowly wink at her. She thought she must have been mistaken, at first, for none of the scarecrows in

Kansas ever wink; but presently the figure nodded its head to her in a friendly way. Then she climbed down from the fence and walked up to it, while Toto ran around the pole and barked.

"Good day," said the Scarecrow, in a rather husky voice.

"Did you speak?" asked the girl, in wonder.

"Certainly," answered the Scarecrow; "how do you do?"

"I'm pretty well, thank you," replied Dorothy, politely; "how do you do?"

"I'm not feeling well," said the Scarecrow, with a smile, "for it is very tedious being perched up here night and day to scare away crows."

"Can't you get down?" asked Dorothy.

"No, for this pole is stuck up my back. If you will please take away the pole I shall be greatly obliged to you."

Dorothy reached up both arms and lifted the figure off the pole; for, being stuffed with straw, it was quite light.

"Thank you very much," said the Scarecrow, when he had been set down on the ground. "I feel like a new man."

Dorothy was puzzled at this, for it sounded queer to hear a stuffed man speak, and to see him bow and walk along beside her.

"Who are you?" asked the Scarecrow, when he had stretched himself and yawned, "and where are you going?"

"My name is Dorothy," said the girl, "and I am going to the Emerald City, to ask the great Oz to send me back to Kansas."

"Where is the Emerald City?" he enquired; "and who is Oz?"

"Why, don't you know?" she returned, in surprise.

"No, indeed; I don't know anything. You see, I am stuffed, so I have no brains at all," he answered, sadly.

"Oh," said Dorothy; "I'm awfully sorry for you."

"Do you think," he asked, "if I go to the Emerald City with you, that the great Oz would give me some brains?"

"I cannot tell," she returned; "but you may come with me, if you like. If Oz will not give you any brains you will be no worse off than you are now."

"That is true," said the Scarecrow. "You see," he continued, confidentially, "I don't mind my legs and arms and body being stuffed, because I cannot get hurt. If anyone treads on my toes or sticks a pin into me, it doesn't matter, for I can't feel it. But I do not want people to call me a fool, and if my head stays stuffed with straw instead of with brains, as yours is, how am I ever to know anything?"

"I understand how you feel," said the little girl, who was truly sorry for him. "If you will come with me I'll ask Oz to do all he can for you."

"Thank you," he answered, gratefully.

They walked back to the road, Dorothy helped him over the fence, and they started along the path of yellow brick for the Emerald City.

Toto did not like this addition to the party, at first. He smelled around the stuffed man as if he suspected there might be a nest of rats in the straw, and he often growled in an unfriendly way at the Scarecrow.

"Don't mind Toto," said Dorothy, to her new friend; "he never bites."

"Oh, I'm not afraid," replied the Scarecrow, "he can't hurt the straw. Do let me carry that basket for you. I shall not mind it, for I can't get tired. I'll tell you a secret," he continued, as he walked along; "there is only one thing in the world I am afraid of."

"What is that?" asked Dorothy; "the Munchkin farmer who made you?"

"No," answered the Scarecrow; "it's a lighted match."

"' I was only made yesterday,' said the Scarecrow."

CHAPTER IV

THE ROAD THROUGH
THE FOREST

A FTER A few hours the road began to be rough, and the walking grew so difficult that the Scarecrow often stumbled over the yellow brick, which were here very uneven. Sometimes, indeed, they were broken or missing altogether, leaving holes that Toto jumped across and Dorothy walked around. As for the Scarecrow, having no brains he walked straight ahead, and so stepped into the holes and fell at full length on the hard bricks. It never hurt him, however, and Dorothy would pick him up and set him upon his feet again, while he joined her in laughing merrily at his own mishap.

The farms were not nearly so well cared for here as they were farther back. There were fewer houses and fewer fruit trees, and the farther they went the more dismal and lonesome the country became.

At noon they sat down by the roadside, near a little brook, and Dorothy opened her basket and got out some bread. She offered a piece to the Scarecrow, but he refused.

"I am never hungry," he said; "and it is a lucky thing I am not. For my mouth is only painted, and if I should cut a hole in it so I could eat, the straw I am stuffed with would come out, and that would spoil the shape of my head."

Dorothy saw at once that this was true, so she only nodded and went on eating her bread.

"Tell me something about yourself, and the country you came from," said the Scarecrow, when she had finished her dinner. So she told him all about Kansas, and how gray everything was there, and how the cyclone had carried her to this queer land of Oz. The Scarecrow listened carefully, and said,

"I cannot understand why you should wish to leave this beautiful country and go back to the dry, gray place you call Kansas."

"That is because you have no brains," answered the girl. "No matter how dreary and gray our homes are, we people of flesh and blood would rather live there than in any other country, be it ever so beautiful. There is no place like home."

The Scarecrow sighed.

"Of course I cannot understand it," he said. "If your heads were stuffed with straw, like mine, you would probably all live in the beautiful places, and then Kansas would have no people at all. It is fortunate for Kansas that you have brains."

"Won't you tell me a story, while we are resting?" asked the child.

The Scarecrow looked at her reproachfully, and answered, "My life has been so short that I really know nothing whatever. I was only made day before yesterday. What happened in the world before that time is all unknown to me. Luckily, when the farmer made my head, one of the first things he did was to paint my ears, so that I heard what was going on. There was another Munchkin with him, and the first thing I heard was the farmer saying,

" 'How do you like those ears?'

" 'They aren't straight,' answered the other.

" 'Never mind,' said the farmer; 'they are ears just the same,' which was true enough.

" 'Now I'll make the eyes,' said the farmer. So he painted my right eye, and as soon as it was finished I found myself looking at him and at everything around me with a great deal of curiosity, for this was my first glimpse of the world.

" 'That's a rather pretty eye,' remarked the Munchkin who was watching the farmer; 'blue paint is just the color for eyes.'

" 'I think I'll make the other a little bigger,' said the farmer; and when the second eye was done I could see much better than before. Then he made my nose and my mouth; but I did not speak, because at that time I didn't know what a mouth was for. I had the fun of watching them make my body and my arms and legs; and when they fastened on my head, at last, I felt very proud, for I thought I was just as good a man as anyone.

" 'This fellow will scare the crows fast enough,' said the farmer; 'he looks just like a man.'

" 'Why, he is a man,' said the other, and I quite agreed with him. The farmer carried me under his arm to the cornfield, and set me up on a tall stick, where you found me. He and his friend soon after walked away and left me alone.

"I did not like to be deserted this way; so I tried to walk after them, but my feet would not touch the ground, and I was forced to stay on that pole. It was a lonely life to lead, for I had nothing to think of, having been made such a little while before. Many crows and other birds flew into the cornfield, but as soon as they saw me they flew away again, thinking I was a Munchkin; and this pleased me and made me feel that I was quite an important person. By and by an old crow flew near me, and after looking at me carefully he perched upon my shoulder and said,

" 'I wonder if that farmer thought to fool me in this clumsy manner. Any crow of sense could see that you are only stuffed with straw.' Then he hopped down at my feet and ate all the corn he wanted. The other birds, seeing he was not harmed by me, came to eat the corn too, so in a short time there was a great flock of them about me.

"I felt sad at this, for it showed I was not such a good Scarecrow after all; but the old crow comforted me, saying: 'If you only had brains in your head you would be as good a man as any of them, and a better man than some of them. Brains are the only things worth having in this world, no matter whether one is a crow or a man.'

"After the crows had gone I thought this over, and decided I would try hard to get some brains. By good luck, you came along and pulled me off the stake, and from what you say I am sure the great Oz will give me brains as soon as we get to the Emerald City."

"I hope so," said Dorothy, earnestly, "since you seem anxious to have them."

"Oh yes; I am anxious," returned the Scarecrow. "It is such an uncomfortable feeling to know one is a fool."

"Well," said the girl, "let us go." And she handed the basket to the Scarecrow.

There were no fences at all by the road side now, and the land was tough and untilled. Towards evening they came to a great forest, where the trees grew so big and close together that their branches met over the road of yellow brick. It was almost dark under the trees, for the branches shut out the daylight; but the travellers did not stop, and went on into the forest.

"If this road goes in, it must come out," said the Scare-crow, "and as the Emerald City is at the other end of the road, we must go wherever it leads us."

"Anyone would know that," said Dorothy.

"Certainly; that is why I know it," returned the Scare-crow. "If it required brains to figure it out, I never should have said it."

After an hour or so the light faded away, and they found themselves stumbling along in the darkness. Dorothy could not see at all, but Toto could, for some dogs see very well in the dark; and the Scarecrow declared he could see as well as by day. So she took hold of his arm, and managed to get along fairly well.

"If you see any house, or any place where we can pass the night," she said, "you must tell me; for it is very uncomfortable walking in the dark."

Soon after the Scarecrow stopped.

"I see a little cottage at the right of us," he said, "built of logs and branches. Shall we go there?"

"Yes, indeed;" answered the child. "I am all tired out."

So the Scarecrow led her through the trees until they reached the cottage, and Dorothy entered and found a bed of dried leaves in one corner. She lay down at once, and with Toto beside her soon fell into a sound sleep. The Scarecrow, who was never tired, stood up in another corner and waited patiently until morning came.

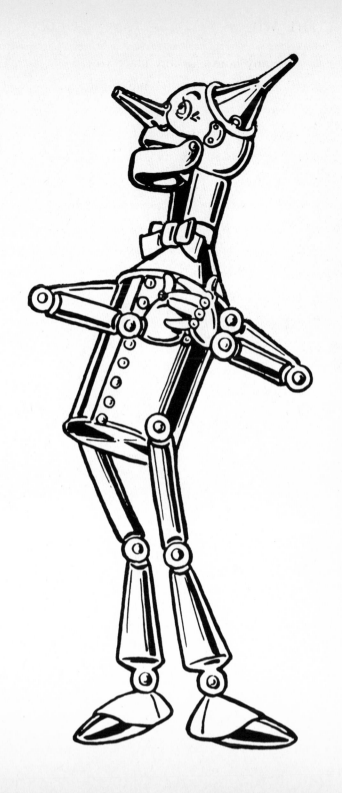

" ' *This is a great comfort,*' *said the Tin Woodman.*"

CHAPTER V

THE RESCUE OF THE TIN WOODMAN

W HEN DOROTHY awoke the sun was shining through the trees and Toto had long been out chasing birds and squirrels. She sat up and looked around her. There was the Scarecrow, still standing patiently in his corner, waiting for her.

"We must go and search for water," she said to him.

"Why do you want water?" he asked.

"To wash my face clean after the dust of the road, and to drink, so the dry bread will not stick in my throat."

"It must be inconvenient to be made of flesh," said the Scarecrow, thoughtfully; "for you must sleep, and eat and drink. However, you have brains, and it is worth a lot of bother to be able to think properly."

They left the cottage and walked through the trees

until they found a little spring of clear water, where Dorothy drank and bathed and ate her breakfast. She saw there was not much bread left in the basket, and the girl was thankful the Scarecrow did not have to eat anything, for there was scarcely enough for herself and Toto for the day.

When she had finished her meal, and was about to go back to the road of yellow brick, she was startled to hear a deep groan near by.

"What was that?" she asked, timidly.

"I cannot imagine," replied the Scarecrow; "but we can go and see."

Just then another groan reached their ears, and the sound seemed to come from behind them. They turned and walked through the forest a few steps, when Dorothy discovered something shining in a ray of sunshine that fell between the trees. She ran to the place, and then stopped short, with a cry of surprise.

One of the big trees had been partly chopped through, and standing beside it, with an uplifted axe in his hands, was a man made entirely of tin. His head and arms and legs were jointed upon his body, but he stood perfectly motionless, as if he could not stir at all.

Dorothy looked at him in amazement, and so did the Scarecrow, while Toto barked sharply and made a snap at the tin legs, which hurt his teeth.

"Did you groan?" asked Dorothy.

"Yes," answered the tin man; "I did. I've been groaning for more than a year, and no one has ever heard me before or come to help me."

"What can I do for you?" she enquired, softly, for she was moved by the sad voice in which the man spoke.

"Get an oil-can and oil my joints," he answered. "They are rusted so badly that I cannot move them at all; if I am well oiled I shall soon be all right again. You will find an oil-can on a shelf in my cottage."

Dorothy at once ran back to the cottage and found the oil-can, and then she returned and asked, anxiously, "Where are your joints?"

"Oil my neck, first," replied the Tin Woodman. So she oiled it, and as it was quite badly rusted the Scarecrow took hold of the tin head and moved it gently from side to side until it worked freely, and then the man could turn it himself.

"Now oil the joints in my arms," he said. And Dorothy oiled them and the Scarecrow bent them carefully until they were quite free from rust and as good as new.

The Tin Woodman gave a sigh of satisfaction and lowered his axe, which he leaned against the tree.

"This is a great comfort," he said. "I have been holding that axe in the air ever since I rusted, and I'm glad to be able to put it down at last. Now, if you will oil the joints of my legs, I shall be all right once more."

So they oiled his legs until he could move them freely; and he thanked them again and again for his release, for he seemed a very polite creature, and very grateful.

"I might have stood there always if you had not come along," he said; "so you have certainly saved my life. How did you happen to be here?"

"We are on our way to the Emerald City, to see the great

Oz," she answered, "and we stopped at your cottage to pass the night."

"Why do you wish to see Oz?" he asked.

"I want him to send me back to Kansas; and the Scarecrow wants him to put a few brains into his head," she replied.

The Tin Woodman appeared to think deeply for a moment. Then he said:

"Do you suppose Oz could give me a heart?"

"Why, I guess so," Dorothy answered; "it would be as easy as to give the Scarecrow brains."

"True," the Tin Woodman returned. "So, if you will allow me to join your party, I will also go to the Emerald City and ask Oz to help me."

"Come along," said the Scarecrow, heartily; and Dorothy added that she would be pleased to have his company. So the Tin Woodman shouldered his axe and they all passed through the forest until they came to the road that was paved with yellow brick.

The Tin Woodman had asked Dorothy to put the oil-can in her basket. "For," he said, "if I should get caught in the rain, and rust again, I would need the oil-can badly."

It was a bit of good luck to have their new comrade join the party, for soon after they had begun their journey again they came to a place where the trees and branches grew so thick over the road that the travellers could not pass. But the Tin Woodman set to work with his axe and chopped so well that soon he cleared a passage for the entire party.

Dorothy was thinking so earnestly as they walked along that she did not notice when the Scarecrow stumbled into a hole and rolled over to the side of the road. Indeed, he was obliged to call to her to help him up again.

"Why didn't you walk around the hole?" asked the Tin Woodman.

"I don't know enough," replied the Scarecrow, cheerfully. "My head is stuffed with straw, you know, and that is why I am going to Oz to ask him for some brains."

"Oh, I see;" said the Tin Woodman. "But, after all, brains are not the best things in the world."

"Have you any?" enquired the Scarecrow.

"No, my head is quite empty," answered the Woodman; "but once I had brains, and a heart also; so, having tried them both, I should much rather have a heart."

"And why is that?" asked the Scarecrow.

"I will tell you my story, and then you will know."

So, while they were walking through the forest, the Tin Woodman told the following story:

"I was born the son of a woodman who chopped down trees in the forest and sold the wood for a living. When I grew up I too became a wood-chopper, and after my father died I took care of my old mother as long as she lived. Then I made up my mind that instead of living alone I would marry, so that I might not become lonely.

"There was one of the Munchkin girls who was so beautiful that I soon grew to love her with all my heart. She, on her part, promised to marry me as soon as I could earn enough money to build a better house for her; so I set to work harder than ever. But the girl lived with an old woman who did not want her to marry anyone, for she was so lazy she wished the girl to remain with her and do the cooking and the housework. So the old woman went to the wicked Witch of the East, and promised her two sheep and a cow if she would prevent the marriage. Thereupon the wicked Witch enchanted my axe, and when I was chopping away at my best one day, for I was anxious to get the new house and my wife as soon as possible, the axe slipped all at once and cut off my left leg.

"This at first seemed a great misfortune, for I knew a one-legged man could not do very well as a wood-chopper. So I went to a tin-smith and had him make me a new leg out of tin. The leg worked very well, once I was used to it; but my action angered the wicked Witch of the East, for she had promised the old woman I should not marry the pretty Munchkin girl. When I began chopping again my axe slipped and cut off my right leg. Again I went to the tinner, and again he made me a leg out of tin. After this the enchanted axe cut off my arms, one after the other; but, nothing daunted, I had them replaced with tin ones. The wicked Witch then made the axe slip and cut off my head, and at first I thought that was the end of me. But the tinner happened to come along, and he made me a new head out of tin.

"I thought I had beaten the wicked Witch then, and I worked harder than ever; but I little knew how cruel my enemy could be. She thought of a new way to kill my love for the beautiful Munchkin maiden, and made my axe slip again, so that it cut right through my body, splitting me into two halves. Once more the tinner came to my help and made me a body of tin, fastening my tin arms and legs and head to it, by means of joints, so that I could move around as well as ever. But, alas! I had now no heart, so that I lost all my love for the Munchkin girl, and did not care whether I married her or not. I suppose she is still living with the old woman, waiting for me to come after her.

"My body shone so brightly in the sun that I felt very proud of it and it did not matter now if my axe slipped, for it could not cut me. There was only one danger—that my joints would rust; but I kept an oil-can in my cottage and took care to oil myself whenever I needed it. However, there came a day when I forgot to do this, and, being caught in a rainstorm, before I thought of the danger my joints had rusted, and I was left to stand in the woods until you came to help me. It was a terrible thing to undergo, but during the year I stood there I had time to think that the greatest loss I had known was the loss of my heart. While I was in love I was the happiest man on earth; but no one can love who has not a heart, and so I am resolved to ask Oz to give me one. If he does, I will go back to the Munchkin maiden and marry her."

Both Dorothy and the Scarecrow had been greatly interested in the story of the Tin Woodman, and now they knew why he was so anxious to get a new heart.

"All the same," said the Scarecrow, "I shall ask for brains instead of a heart; for a fool would not know what to do with a heart if he had one."

"I shall take the heart," returned the Tin Woodman; "for brains do not make one happy, and happiness is the best thing in the world."

Dorothy did not say anything, for she was puzzled to know which of her two friends was right, and she decided if she could only get back to Kansas and Aunt Em it did not matter so much whether the Woodman had no brains and the Scarecrow no heart, or each got what he wanted.

What worried her most was that the bread was nearly gone, and another meal for herself and Toto would empty the basket. To be sure neither the Woodman nor the Scarecrow ever ate anything, but she was not made of tin nor straw, and could not live unless she was fed.

" You ought to be ashamed of yourself ! "

CHAPTER VI

THE COWARDLY LION

ALL THIS time Dorothy and her companions had been walking through the thick woods. The road was still paved with yellow brick, but these were much covered by dried branches and dead leaves from the trees, and the walking was not at all good.

There were few birds in this part of the forest, for birds love the open country where there is plenty of sunshine; but now and then there came a deep growl from some wild animal hidden among the trees. These sounds made the little girl's heart beat fast, for she did not know what made them; but Toto knew, and he walked close to Dorothy's side, and did not even bark in return.

"How long will it be," the child asked of the Tin Woodman, "before we are out of the forest?"

"I cannot tell," was the answer, "for I have never been to the Emerald City. But my father went there once, when I was a boy, and he said it was a long journey through a dangerous country, although nearer to the city where Oz dwells the country is beautiful. But I am not afraid so long as I have my oil-can, and nothing can hurt the Scarecrow, while you bear upon your forehead the mark of the good Witch's kiss, and that will protect you from harm."

"But Toto!" said the girl, anxiously; "what will protect him?"

"We must protect him ourselves, if he is in danger," replied the Tin Woodman.

Just as he spoke there came from the forest a terrible roar, and the next moment a great Lion bounded into the road. With one blow of his paw he sent the Scarecrow spinning over and over to the edge of the road, and then he struck at the Tin Woodman with his sharp claws. But, to the Lion's surprise, he could make no impression on the tin, although the Woodman fell over in the road and lay still.

Little Toto, now that he had an enemy to face, ran barking toward the Lion, and the great beast had opened his mouth to bite the dog, when Dorothy, fearing Toto would be killed, and heedless of danger, rushed forward and slapped the Lion upon his nose as hard as she could, while she cried out:

"Don't you dare to bite Toto! You ought to be ashamed of yourself, a big beast like you, to bite a poor little dog!"

"I didn't bite him," said the Lion, as he rubbed his nose with his paw where Dorothy had hit it.

"No, but you tried to," she retorted. "You are nothing but a big coward."

"I know it," said the Lion, hanging his head in shame; "I've always known it. But how can I help it?"

"I don't know, I'm sure. To think of your striking a stuffed man, like the poor Scarecrow!"

"Is he stuffed?" asked the Lion, in surprise, as he watched her pick up the Scarecrow and set him upon his feet, while she patted him into shape again.

"Of course he's stuffed," replied Dorothy, who was still angry.

"That's why he went over so easily," remarked the Lion. "It astonished me to see him whirl around so. Is the other one stuffed, also?"

"No," said Dorothy, "he's made of tin." And she helped the Woodman up again.

"That's why he nearly blunted my claws," said the Lion. "When they scratched against the tin it made a cold shiver run down my back. What is that little animal you are so tender of?"

"He is my dog, Toto," answered Dorothy.

"Is he made of tin, or stuffed?" asked the Lion.

"Neither. He's a—a—a meat dog," said the girl.

"Oh. He's a curious animal, and seems remarkably small, now that I look at him. No one would think of biting such a little thing except a coward like me," continued the Lion, sadly.

"What makes you a coward?" asked Dorothy, looking at the great beast in wonder, for he was as big as a small horse.

"It's a mystery," replied the Lion. "I suppose I was born that way. All the other animals in the forest naturally expect me to be brave, for the Lion is everywhere thought to be the King of Beasts. I learned that if I roared very loudly every living thing was frightened and got out of my way. Whenever I've met a man I've been awfully scared; but I just roared at him, and he has always run away as fast as he could go. If the elephants and the tigers and the bears had ever tried to fight me, I should have run myself—I'm such a coward; but just as soon as they hear me roar they all try to get away from me, and of course I let them go."

"But that isn't right. The King of Beasts shouldn't be a coward," said the Scarecrow.

"I know it," returned the Lion, wiping a tear from his eye with the tip of his tail; "it is my great sorrow, and makes my life very unhappy. But whenever there is danger my heart begins to beat fast."

"Perhaps you have heart disease," said the Tin Woodman.

"It may be," said the Lion.

"If you have," continued the Tin Woodman, "you ought to be glad, for it proves you have a heart. For my part, I have no heart; so I cannot have heart disease."

"Perhaps," said the Lion, thoughtfully, "if I had no heart I should not be a coward."

"Have you brains?" asked the Scarecrow.

"I suppose so. I've never looked to see," replied the Lion.

"I am going to the great Oz to ask him to give me some," remarked the Scarecrow, "for my head is stuffed with straw."

"And I am going to ask him to give me a heart," said the Woodman.

"And I am going to ask him to send Toto and me back to Kansas," added Dorothy.

"Do you think Oz could give me courage?" asked the Cowardly Lion.

"Just as easily as he could give me brains," said the Scarecrow.

"Or give me a heart," said the Tin Woodman.

"Or send me back to Kansas," said Dorothy.

"Then, if you don't mind, I'll go with you," said the Lion, "for my life is simply unbearable without a bit of courage."

"You will be very welcome," answered Dorothy, "for you will help to keep away the other wild beasts. It seems to me they must be more cowardly than you are if they allow you to scare them so easily."

"They really are," said the Lion; "but that doesn't make me any braver, and as long as I know myself to be a coward I shall be unhappy."

So once more the little company set off upon the journey, the Lion walking with stately strides at Dorothy's side. Toto did not approve this new comrade at first, for he could not forget how nearly he had been crushed between the Lion's great jaws; but after a time he became more at ease, and presently Toto and the Cowardly Lion had grown to be good friends.

During the rest of that day there was no other adventure to mar the peace of their journey. Once, indeed, the Tin Woodman stepped upon a beetle that was crawling along the road, and killed the poor little thing. This made the Tin Woodman very unhappy, for he was always careful not to hurt any living creature; and as he walked along he wept several tears of sorrow and regret. These tears ran slowly down his face and over the hinges of his jaw, and there they rusted. When Dorothy presently asked him a question the Tin Woodman could not open his mouth, for his jaws were tightly rusted together. He became greatly frightened at this and made many motions to Dorothy to relieve him, but she could not understand. The Lion was also puzzled to know what was wrong. But the Scarecrow seized the oil-can from Dorothy's basket and oiled the Woodman's jaws, so that after a few moments he could talk as well as before.

"This will serve me a lesson," said he, "to look where I step. For if I should kill another bug or beetle I should surely cry again, and crying rusts my jaw so that I cannot speak."

Thereafter he walked very carefully, with his eyes on the road, and when he saw a tiny ant toiling by he would step over it, so as not to harm it. The Tin Woodman knew very well he had no heart, and therefore he took great care never to be cruel or unkind to anything.

"You people with hearts," he said, "have something to guide you, and need never do wrong; but I have no heart, and so I must be very careful. When Oz gives me a heart of course I needn't mind so much."

" The tree fell with a crash into the gulf."

CHAPTER VII

THE JOURNEY TO THE GREAT OZ

THEY WERE obliged to camp out that night under a large tree in the forest, for there were no houses near. The tree made a good, thick covering to protect them from the dew, and the Tin Woodman chopped a great pile of wood with his axe and Dorothy built a splendid fire that warmed her and made her feel less lonely. She and Toto ate the last of their bread, and now she did not know what they would do for breakfast.

"If you wish," said the Lion, "I will go into the forest and kill a deer for you. You can roast it by the fire, since your tastes are so peculiar that you prefer cooked food, and then you will have a very good breakfast."

"Don't! please don't," begged the Tin Woodman. "I should certainly weep if you killed a poor deer, and then my jaws would rust again."

But the Lion went away into the forest and found his own supper, and no one ever knew what it was, for he didn't mention it. And the Scarecrow found a tree full of nuts and filled Dorothy's basket with them, so that she would not be hungry for a long time. She thought this was very kind and thoughtful of the Scarecrow, but she laughed heartily at the awkward way in which the poor creature picked up the nuts. His padded hands were so clumsy and the nuts were so small that he dropped almost as many as he put in the basket. But the Scarecrow did not mind how long it took him to fill the basket, for it enabled him to keep away from the fire, as he feared a spark might get into his straw and burn him up. So he kept a good distance away from the flames, and only came near to cover Dorothy with dry leaves when she lay down to sleep. These kept her very snug and warm and she slept soundly until morning.

When it was daylight the girl bathed her face in a little rippling brook and soon after they all started toward the Emerald City.

This was to be an eventful day for the travellers. They had hardly been walking an hour when they saw before them a great ditch that crossed the road and divided the forest as far as they could see on either side. It was a very wide ditch, and when they crept up to the edge and looked into it they could see it was also very deep, and there were many big, jagged rocks at the bottom. The sides were so steep that none of them could climb down, and for a moment it seemed that their journey must end.

"What shall we do?" asked Dorothy, despairingly.

"I haven't the faintest idea," said the Tin Woodman; and

the Lion shook his shaggy mane and looked thoughtful. But the Scarecrow said:

"We cannot fly, that is certain; neither can we climb down into this great ditch. Therefore, if we cannot jump over it, we must stop where we are."

"I think I could jump over it," said the Cowardly Lion, after measuring the distance carefully in his mind.

"Then we are all right," answered the Scarecrow, "for you can carry us all over on your back, one at a time."

"Well, I'll try it," said the Lion. "Who will go first?"

"I will," declared the Scarecrow; "for, if you found that you could not jump over the gulf, Dorothy would be killed, or the Tin Woodman badly dented on the rocks below. But if I am on your back it will not matter so much, for the fall would not hurt me at all."

"I am terribly afraid of falling, myself," said the Cowardly Lion, "but I suppose there is nothing to do but try it. So get on my back and we will make the attempt."

The Scarecrow sat upon the Lion's back, and the big beast walked to the edge of the gulf and crouched down.

"Why don't you run and jump?" asked the Scarecrow.

"Because that isn't the way we Lions do these things," he replied. Then giving a great spring, he shot through the air and landed safely on the other side. They were all greatly pleased to see how easily he did it, and after the Scarecrow had got down from his back the Lion sprang across the ditch again.

Dorothy thought she would go next; so she took Toto in her arms and climbed on the Lion's back, holding tightly to his mane with one hand. The next moment it seemed as if she was flying through the air; and then, before she had time to think about it, she was safe on the other side. The Lion went back a third time and got the Tin Woodman, and then they all sat down for a few moments to give the beast a chance to rest, for his great leaps had made his breath short, and he panted like a big dog that has been running too long.

They found the forest very thick on this side, and it looked dark and gloomy. After the Lion had rested they started along the road of yellow brick, silently wondering, each in his own mind, if ever they would come to the end of the woods and reach the bright sunshine again. To add to their discomfort, they soon heard strange noises in the depths of the forest, and the Lion whispered to them that it was in this part of the country that the Kalidahs lived.

"What are the Kalidahs?" asked the girl.

"They are monstrous beasts with bodies like bears and heads like tigers," replied the Lion; "and with claws so long and sharp that they could tear me in two as easily as I could kill Toto. I'm terribly afraid of the Kalidahs."

"I am not surprised that you are," returned Dorothy. "They must be dreadful beasts."

The Lion was about to reply when suddenly they came to another gulf across the road; but this one was so broad and deep that the Lion knew at once he could not leap across it.

So they sat down to consider what they should do, and after serious thought the Scarecrow said,

"Here is a great tree, standing close to the ditch. If the Tin Woodman can chop it down, so that it will fall to the other side, we can walk across it easily."

"That is a first rate idea," said the Lion. "One would almost suspect you had brains in your head, instead of straw."

The Woodman set to work at once, and so sharp was his axe that the tree was soon chopped nearly through. Then the Lion put his strong front legs against the tree and pushed with all his might, and slowly the big tree tipped and fell with a crash across the ditch, with its top branches on the other side.

They had just started to cross this queer bridge when a sharp growl made them all look up, and to their horror they saw running toward them two great beasts with bodies like bears and heads like tigers.

"They are the Kalidahs!" said the Cowardly Lion, beginning to tremble.

"Quick!" cried the Scarecrow, "let us cross over."

So Dorothy went first, holding Toto in her arms; the Tin Woodman followed, and the Scarecrow came next. The Lion, although he was certainly afraid, turned to face the Kalidahs, and then he gave so loud and terrible a roar that Dorothy screamed and the Scarecrow fell over backwards, while even the fierce beasts stopped short and looked at him in surprise.

But, seeing they were bigger than the Lion, and remembering that there were two of them and only one of him, the Kalidahs again rushed forward, and the Lion crossed over the tree and turned to see what they would do next. Without stopping an instant the fierce beasts also began to cross the tree, and the Lion said to Dorothy,

"We are lost, for they will surely tear us to pieces with

their sharp claws. But stand close behind me, and I will fight them as long as I am alive."

"Wait a minute!" called the Scarecrow. He had been thinking what was best to be done, and now he asked the Woodman to chop away the end of the tree that rested on their side of the ditch. The Tin Woodman began to use his axe at once, and, just as the two Kalidahs were nearly across, the tree fell with a crash into the gulf, carrying the ugly, snarling brutes with it, and both were dashed to pieces on the sharp rocks at the bottom.

"Well," said the Cowardly Lion, drawing a long breath of relief, "I see we are going to live a little while longer, and I am glad of it, for it must be a very uncomfortable thing not to be alive. Those creatures frightened me so badly that my heart is beating yet."

"Ah." said the Tin Woodman, sadly, "I wish I had a heart to beat."

This adventure made the travellers more anxious than ever to get out of the forest, and they walked so fast that Dorothy became tired, and had to ride on the Lion's back. To their great joy the trees became thinner the further they advanced, and in the afternoon they suddenly came upon a broad river, flowing swiftly just before them. On the other side of the water they could see the road of yellow brick running through a beautiful country, with green meadows dotted with bright flowers and all the road bordered with trees hanging full of delicious fruits. They were greatly pleased to see this delightful country before them.

"How shall we cross the river?" asked Dorothy.

"That is easily done," replied the Scarecrow. "The Tin

Woodman must build us a raft, so we can float to the other side."

So the Woodman took his axe and began to chop down small trees to make a raft, and while he was busy at this the Scarecrow found on the river bank a tree full of fine fruit. This pleased Dorothy, who had eaten nothing but nuts all day, and she made a hearty meal of the ripe fruit.

But it takes time to make a raft, even when one is as industrious and untiring as the Tin Woodman, and when night came the work was not done. So they found a cozy place under the trees where they slept well until the morning; and Dorothy dreamed of the Emerald City, and of the good Wizard Oz, who would soon send her back to her own home again.

" The Stork carried him up into the air."

CHAPTER VIII

THE DEADLY
POPPY FIELD

OUR LITTLE party of travellers awakened next morning refreshed and full of hope, and Dorothy breakfasted like a princess off peaches and plums from the trees beside the river.

Behind them was the dark forest they had passed safely through, although they had suffered many discouragements; but before them was a lovely, sunny country that seemed to beckon them on to the Emerald City.

To be sure, the broad river now cut them off from this beautiful land; but the raft was nearly done, and after the Tin Woodman had cut a few more logs and fastened them together with wooden pins, they were ready to start. Dorothy sat down in the middle of the raft and held Toto in her arms. When the Cowardly Lion stepped upon the raft it tipped badly, for he was big and heavy; but the Scarecrow and the Tin Woodman stood upon the other end to steady it, and they had long poles in their hands to push the raft through the water.

They got along quite well at first, but when they reached the middle of the river the swift current swept the raft down stream, farther and farther away from the road of yellow brick; and the water grew so deep that the long poles would not touch the bottom.

"This is bad," said the Tin Woodman, "for if we cannot get to the land we shall be carried into the country of the wicked Witch of the West, and she will enchant us and make us her slaves."

"And then I should get no brains," said the Scarecrow.

"And I should get no courage," said the Cowardly Lion.

"And I should get no heart," said the Tin Woodman.

"And I should never get back to Kansas," said Dorothy.

"We must certainly get to the Emerald City if we can," the Scarecrow continued, and he pushed so hard on his long pole that it stuck fast in the mud at the bottom of the river, and before he could pull it out again, or let go, the raft was swept away and the poor Scarecrow left clinging to the pole in the middle of the river.

"Good bye!" he called after them, and they were very sorry to leave him; indeed, the Tin Woodman began to cry, but fortunately remembered that he might rust, and so dried his tears on Dorothy's apron.

Of course this was a bad thing for the Scarecrow.

"I am now worse off than when I first met Dorothy," he

thought. "Then, I was stuck on a pole in a cornfield, where I could make believe scare the crows, at any rate; but surely there is no use for a Scarecrow stuck on a pole in the middle of a river. I am afraid I shall never have any brains, after all!"

Down the stream the raft floated, and the poor Scarecrow was left far behind. Then the Lion said:

"Something must be done to save us. I think I can swim to the shore and pull the raft after me, if you will only hold fast to the tip of my tail."

So he sprang into the water and the Tin Woodman caught fast hold of his tail, when the Lion began to swim with all his might toward the shore. It was hard work, although he was so big; but by and by they were drawn out of the current, and then Dorothy took the Tin Woodman's long pole and helped push the raft to the land.

They were all tired out when they reached the shore at last and stepped off upon the pretty green grass, and they also knew that the stream had carried them a long way past the road of yellow brick that led to the Emerald City.

"What shall we do now?" asked the Tin Woodman, as the Lion lay down on the grass to let the sun dry him.

"We must get back to the road, in some way," said Dorothy.

"The best plan will be to walk along the river bank until we come to the road again," remarked the Lion.

So, when they were rested, Dorothy picked up her basket and they started along the grassy bank, back to the road from which the river had carried them. It was a lovely country, with plenty of flowers and fruit trees and sunshine to cheer them, and had they not felt so sorry for the poor Scarecrow they could have been very happy.

They walked along as fast as they could, Dorothy only stopping once to pick a beautiful flower; and after a time the Tin Woodman cried out,

"Look!"

Then they all looked at the river and saw the Scarecrow perched upon his pole in the middle of the water, looking very lonely and sad.

"What can we do to save him?" asked Dorothy.

The Lion and the Woodman both shook their heads, for they did not know. So they sat down upon the bank and gazed wistfully at the Scarecrow until a Stork flew by, which, seeing them, stopped to rest at the water's edge.

"Who are you, and where are you going?" asked the Stork.

"I am Dorothy," answered the girl; "and these are my friends, the Tin Woodman and the Cowardly Lion; and we are going to the Emerald City."

"This isn't the road," said the Stork, as she twisted her long neck and looked sharply at the queer party.

"I know it," returned Dorothy, "but we have lost the Scarecrow, and are wondering how we shall get him again."

"Where is he?" asked the Stork.

"Over there in the river," answered the girl.

"If he wasn't so big and heavy I would get him for you," remarked the Stork.

"He isn't heavy a bit," said Dorothy, eagerly, "for he is

stuffed with straw; and if you will bring him back to us we shall thank you ever and ever so much."

"Well, I'll try," said the Stork; "but if I find he is too heavy to carry I shall have to drop him in the river again."

So the big bird flew into the air and over the water till she came to where the Scarecrow was perched upon his pole. Then the Stork with her great claws grabbed the Scarecrow by the arm and carried him up into the air and back to the bank, where Dorothy and the Lion and the Tin Woodman and Toto were sitting.

When the Scarecrow found himself among his friends again he was so happy that he hugged them all, even the Lion and Toto; and as they walked along he sang "Tol-de-ri-de-oh!" at every step, he felt so gay.

"I was afraid I should have to stay in the river forever," he said, "but the kind Stork saved me, and if I ever get any brains I shall find the Stork again and do it some kindness in return."

"That's all right," said the Stork, who was flying along beside them. "I always like to help anyone in trouble. But I must go now, for my babies are waiting in the nest for me. I hope you will find the Emerald City and that Oz will help you."

"Thank you," replied Dorothy, and then the kind Stork flew into the air and was soon out of sight.

They walked along listening to the singing of the bright-colored birds and looking at the lovely flowers which now became so thick that the ground was carpeted with them. There were big yellow and white and blue and purple blossoms, besides great clusters of scarlet poppies, which were so brilliant in color they almost dazzled Dorothy's eyes.

"Aren't they beautiful?" the girl asked, as she breathed in the spicy scent of the flowers.

"I suppose so," answered the Scarecrow. "When I have brains I shall probably like them better."

"If I only had a heart I should love them," added the Tin Woodman.

"I always did like flowers," said the Lion; "they seem so helpless and frail. But there are none in the forest so bright as these."

They now came upon more and more of the big scarlet poppies, and fewer and fewer of the other flowers; and soon they found themselves in the midst of a great meadow of poppies. Now it is well known that when there are many of these flowers together their odor is so powerful that anyone who breathes it falls asleep, and if the sleeper is not carried away from the scene of the flowers he sleeps on and on forever. But Dorothy did not know this, nor could she get away from the bright red flowers that were everywhere about; so presently her eyes grew heavy and she felt she must sit down to rest and to sleep.

But the Tin Woodman would not let her do this.

"We must hurry and get back to the road of yellow brick before dark," he said; and the Scarecrow agreed with him. So they kept walking until Dorothy could stand no longer. Her eyes closed in spite of herself and she forgot where she was and fell among the poppies, fast asleep.

"What shall we do?" asked the Tin Woodman.

"If we leave her here she will die," said the Lion. "The smell of the flowers is killing us all. I myself can scarcely keep my eyes open and the dog is asleep already."

It was true; Toto had fallen down beside his little mistress. But the Scarecrow and the Tin Woodman, not being made of flesh, were not troubled by the scent of the flowers.

"Run fast," said the Scarecrow to the Lion, "and get out of this deadly flower-bed as soon as you can. We will bring the little girl with us, but if you should fall asleep you are too big to be carried."

So the Lion aroused himself and bounded forward as fast as he could go. In a moment he was out of sight.

"Let us make a chair with our hands, and carry her," said the Scarecrow. So they picked up Toto and put the dog in Dorothy's lap, and then they made a chair with their hands for the seat and their arms for the arms and carried the sleeping girl between them through the flowers.

On and on they walked, and it seemed that the great carpet of deadly flowers that surrounded them would never end. They followed the bend of the river, and at last came upon their friend the Lion, lying fast asleep among the poppies. The flowers had been too strong for the huge beast and he had given up, at last, and fallen only a short distance from the end of the poppy-bed, where the sweet grass spread in beautiful green fields before them.

"We can do nothing for him," said the Tin Woodman, sadly; "for he is much too heavy to lift. We must leave him here to sleep on forever, and perhaps he will dream that he has found courage at last."

"I'm sorry," said the Scarecrow; "the Lion was a very good comrade for one so cowardly. But let us go on."

They carried the sleeping girl to a pretty spot beside the river, far enough from the poppy field to prevent her breathing any more of the poison of the flowers, and here they laid her gently on the soft grass and waited for the fresh breeze to waken her.

"Permit me to introduce to you her Majesty, the Queen."

CHAPTER IX

THE QUEEN OF
THE FIELD-MICE

"WE CANNOT be far from the road of yellow brick, now," remarked the Scarecrow, as he stood beside the girl, "for we have come nearly as far as the river carried us away."

The Tin Woodman was about to reply when he heard a low growl, and turning his head (which worked beautifully on hinges) he saw a strange beast come bounding over the grass towards them. It was, indeed, a great, yellow wildcat, and the Woodman thought it must be chasing something, for its ears were lying close to its head and its mouth was wide open, showing two rows of ugly teeth, while its red eyes glowed like balls of fire. As it came nearer the Tin Woodman saw that running before the beast was a little gray field-mouse, and although he had no heart he knew it

165

was wrong for the wildcat to try to kill such a pretty, harmless creature.

So the Woodman raised his axe, and as the wildcat ran by he gave it a quick blow that cut the beast's head clean off from its body, and it rolled over at his feet in two pieces.

The field-mouse, now that it was freed from its enemy, stopped short; and coming slowly up to the Woodman it said, in a squeaky little voice,

"Oh, thank you! Thank you ever so much for saving my life."

"Don't speak of it, I beg of you," replied the Woodman. "I have no heart, you know, so I am careful to help all those who may need a friend, even if it happens to be only a mouse."

"Only a mouse!" cried the little animal, indignantly; "why, I am a Queen—the Queen of all the field-mice!"

"Oh, indeed," said the Woodman, making a bow.

"Therefore you have done a great deed, as well as a brave one, in saving my life," added the Queen.

At that moment several mice were seen running up as fast as their little legs could carry them, and when they saw their Queen they exclaimed,

"Oh, your Majesty, we thought you would be killed! How did you manage to escape the great Wildcat?" and they all bowed so low to the little Queen that they almost stood upon their heads.

"This funny tin man," she answered, "killed the wildcat and saved my life. So hereafter you must all serve him, and obey his slightest wish."

"We will!" cried all the mice, in a shrill chorus. And then

they scampered in all directions, for Toto had awakened from his sleep, and seeing all these mice around him he gave one bark of delight and jumped right into the middle of the group. Toto had always loved to chase mice when he lived in Kansas, and he saw no harm in it.

But the Tin Woodman caught the dog in his arms and held him tight, while he called to the mice: "Come back! come back! Toto shall not hurt you."

At this the Queen of the Mice stuck her head out from a clump of grass and asked, in a timid voice,

"Are you sure he will not bite us?"

"I will not let him," said the Woodman; "so do not be afraid."

One by one the mice came creeping back, and Toto did not bark again, although he tried to get out of the Woodman's arms, and would have bitten him had he not known very well he was made of tin. Finally one of the biggest mice spoke.

"Is there anything we can do," it asked, "to repay you for saving the life of our Queen?"

"Nothing that I know of," answered the Woodman; but the Scarecrow, who had been trying to think, but could not because his head was stuffed with straw, said, quickly,

"Oh, yes; you can save our friend, the Cowardly Lion, who is asleep in the poppy bed."

"A Lion!" cried the little Queen; "why, he would eat us all up."

"Oh, no;" declared the Scarecrow; "this Lion is a coward."

"Really?" asked the Mouse.

"He says so himself," answered the Scarecrow, "and he would never hurt anyone who is our friend. If you will help us to save him I promise that he shall treat you all with kindness."

"Very well," said the Queen, "we will trust you. But what shall we do?"

"Are there many of these mice which call you Queen and are willing to obey you?"

"Oh, yes; there are thousands," she replied.

"Then send for them all to come here as soon as possible, and let each one bring a long piece of string."

The Queen turned to the mice that attended her and told them to go at once and get all her people. As soon as they heard her orders they ran away in every direction as fast as possible.

"Now," said the Scarecrow to the Tin Woodman, "you must go to those trees by the river-side and make a truck that will carry the Lion."

So the Woodman went at once to the trees and began to work; and he soon made a truck out of the limbs of trees, from which he chopped away all the leaves and branches. He fastened it together with wooden pegs and made the four wheels out of short pieces of a big tree-trunk. So fast and so well did he work that by the time the mice began to arrive the truck was all ready for them.

They came from all directions, and there were thousands of them: big mice and little mice and middle-sized mice; and each one brought a piece of string in his mouth. It was about this time that Dorothy woke from her long sleep and opened her eyes. She was greatly astonished to find herself lying upon the grass, with thousands of mice standing around and looking at her timidly. But the Scarecrow told her about everything, and turning to the dignified little Mouse, he said,

"Permit me to introduce to you her Majesty, the Queen."

Dorothy nodded gravely and the Queen made a curtsey, after which she became quite friendly with the little girl.

The Scarecrow and the Woodman now began to fasten the mice to the truck, using the strings they had brought. One end of a string was tied around the neck of each mouse and the other end to the truck. Of course the truck was a thousand times bigger than any of the mice who were to draw it; but when all the mice had been harnessed they were able to pull it quite easily. Even the Scarecrow and the Tin Woodman could sit on it, and were drawn swiftly by their queer little horses to the place where the Lion lay asleep.

After a great deal of hard work, for the Lion was heavy, they managed to get him up on the truck. Then the Queen hurriedly gave her people the order to start, for she feared if the mice stayed among the poppies too long they also would fall asleep.

At first the little creatures, many though they were, could hardly stir the heavily loaded truck; but the Woodman and the Scarecrow both pushed from behind, and they got along better. Soon they rolled the Lion out of the poppy bed to the green fields, where he could breathe the sweet, fresh air again, instead of the poisonous scent of the flowers.

Dorothy came to meet them and thanked the little mice warmly for saving her companion from death. She had grown so fond of the big Lion she was glad he had been rescued.

Then the mice were unharnessed from the truck and scampered away through the grass to their homes. The Queen of the Mice was the last to leave.

"If ever you need us again," she said, "come out into the field and call, and we shall hear you and come to your assistance. Good bye!"

"Good bye!" they all answered, and away the Queen ran, while Dorothy held Toto tightly lest he should run after her and frighten her.

After this they sat down beside the Lion until he should awaken; and the Scarecrow brought Dorothy some fruit from a tree near by, which she ate for her dinner.

" The Lion ate some of the porridge."

CHAPTER X

THE GUARDIAN OF THE GATES

I T WAS some time before the Cowardly Lion awakened, for he had lain among the poppies a long while, breathing in their deadly fragrance; but when he did open his eyes and roll off the truck he was very glad to find himself still alive.

"I ran as fast as I could," he said, sitting down and yawning; "but the flowers were too strong for me. How did you get me out?"

Then they told him of the field-mice, and how they had generously saved him from death; and the Cowardly Lion laughed, and said,

"I have always thought myself very big and terrible; yet such small things as flowers came near to killing me, and such small animals as mice have saved my life. How strange it all is! But, comrades, what shall we do now?"

"We must journey on until we find the road of yellow brick again," said Dorothy; "and then we can keep on to the Emerald City."

So, the Lion being fully refreshed, and feeling quite himself again, they all started upon the journey, greatly enjoying the walk through the soft, fresh grass; and it was not long before they reached the road of yellow brick and turned again toward the Emerald City where the great Oz dwelt.

The road was smooth and well paved, now, and the country about was beautiful; so that the travellers rejoiced in leaving the forest far behind, and with it the many dangers they had met in its gloomy shades. Once more they could see fences built beside the road; but these were painted green, and when they came to a small house, in which a farmer evidently lived, that also was painted green. They passed by several of these houses during the afternoon, and sometimes people came to the doors and looked at them as if they would like to ask questions; but no one came near them nor spoke to them because of the great Lion, of which they were much afraid. The people were all dressed in clothing of a lovely emerald green color and wore peaked hats like those of the Munchkins.

"This must be the Land of Oz," said Dorothy, "and we are surely getting near the Emerald City."

"Yes," answered the Scarecrow; "everything is green here, while in the country of the Munchkins blue was the favorite color. But the people do not seem to be as friendly as the Munchkins and I'm afraid we shall be unable to find a place to pass the night."

"I should like something to eat besides fruit," said the girl, "and I'm sure Toto is nearly starved. Let us stop at the next house and talk to the people."

So, when they came to a good sized farm house, Dorothy walked boldly up to the door and knocked. A woman opened it just far enough to look out, and said,

"What do you want, child, and why is that great Lion with you?"

"We wish to pass the night with you, if you will allow us," answered Dorothy; "and the Lion is my friend and comrade, and would not hurt you for the world."

"Is he tame?" asked the woman, opening the door a little wider.

"Oh, yes;" said the girl, "and he is a great coward, too; so that he will be more afraid of you than you are of him."

"Well," said the woman, after thinking it over and taking another peep at the Lion, "if that is the case you may come in, and I will give you some supper and a place to sleep."

So they all entered the house, where there were, besides the woman, two children and a man. The man had hurt his leg, and was lying on the couch in a corner. They seemed greatly surprised to see so strange a company, and while the woman was busy laying the table the man asked,

"Where are you all going?"

"To the Emerald City," said Dorothy, "to see the Great Oz."

"Oh, indeed!" exclaimed the man. "Are you sure that Oz will see you?"

"Why not?" she replied.

"Why, it is said that he never lets any one come into his presence. I have been to the Emerald City many times, and it is a beautiful and wonderful place; but I have never been permitted to see the Great Oz, nor do I know of any living person who has seen him."

"Does he never go out?" asked the Scarecrow.

"Never. He sits day after day in the great throne room of his palace, and even those who wait upon him do not see him face to face."

"What is he like?" asked the girl.

"That is hard to tell," said the man, thoughtfully. "You see, Oz is a great Wizard, and can take on any form he wishes. So that some say he looks like a bird; and some say he looks like an elephant; and some say he looks like a cat. To others he appears as a beautiful fairy, or a brownie, or in any other form that pleases him. But who the real Oz is, when he is in his own form, no living person can tell."

"That is very strange," said Dorothy; "but we must try, in some way, to see him, or we shall have made our journey for nothing."

"Why do you wish to see the terrible Oz?" asked the man.

"I want him to give me some brains," said the Scarecrow, eagerly.

"Oh, Oz could do that easily enough," declared the man. "He has more brains than he needs."

"And I want him to give me a heart," said the Tin Woodman.

"That will not trouble him," continued the man, "for Oz has a large collection of hearts, of all sizes and shapes."

"And I want him to give me courage," said the Cowardly Lion.

"Oz keeps a great pot of courage in his throne room," said the man, "which he has covered with a golden plate, to keep it from running over. He will be glad to give you some."

"And I want him to send me back to Kansas," said Dorothy.

"Where is Kansas?" asked the man, in surprise.

"I don't know," replied Dorothy, sorrowfully; "but it is my home, and I'm sure it's somewhere."

"Very likely. Well, Oz can do anything; so I suppose he will find Kansas for you. But first you must get to see him, and that will be a hard task; for the great Wizard does not like to see anyone, and he usually has his own way. But what do YOU want?" he continued, speaking to Toto. Toto only wagged his tail; for, strange to say, he could not speak.

The woman now called to them that supper was ready, so they gathered around the table and Dorothy ate some delicious porridge and a dish of scrambled eggs and a plate of nice white bread, and enjoyed her meal. The Lion ate some of the porridge, but did not care for it, saying it was made from oats and oats were food for horses, not for lions. The Scarecrow and the Tin Woodman ate nothing at all. Toto ate a little of everything, and was glad to get a good supper again.

The woman now gave Dorothy a bed to sleep in, and Toto lay down beside her, while the Lion guarded the door of her room so she might not be disturbed. The Scarecrow and the Tin Woodman stood up in a corner and kept quiet all night, although of course they could not sleep.

The next morning, as soon as the sun was up, they started on their way, and soon saw a beautiful green glow in the sky just before them.

"That must be the Emerald City," said Dorothy.

As they walked on, the green glow became brighter and brighter, and it seemed that at last they were nearing the end of their travels. Yet it was afternoon before they came to the great wall that surrounded the City. It was high, and thick, and of a bright green color.

In front of them, and at the end of the road of yellow brick, was a big gate, all studded with emeralds that glittered so in the sun that even the painted eyes of the Scarecrow were dazzled by their brilliancy.

There was a bell beside the gate, and Dorothy pushed the button and heard a silvery tinkle sound within. Then the big gate swung slowly open, and they all passed through and found themselves in a high arched room, the walls of which glistened with countless emeralds.

Before them stood a little man about the same size as the Munchkins. He was clothed all in green, from his head to his feet, and even his skin was of a greenish tint. At his side was a large green box.

When he saw Dorothy and her companions the man asked,

"What do you wish in the Emerald City?"

"We came here to see the Great Oz," said Dorothy.

The man was so surprised at this answer that he sat down to think it over.

"It has been many years since anyone asked me to see Oz," he said, shaking his head in perplexity. "He is powerful and terrible, and if you come on an idle or foolish errand to bother the wise reflections of the Great Wizard, he might be angry and destroy you all in an instant."

"But it is not a foolish errand, nor an idle one," replied the Scarecrow; "it is important. And we have been told that Oz is a good Wizard."

"So he is," said the green man; "and he rules the Emerald City wisely and well. But to those who are not honest, or who approach him from curiosity, he is most terrible, and few have ever dared ask to see his face. I am the Guardian of the Gates, and since you demand to see the Great Oz I must take you to his palace. But first you must put on the spectacles."

"Why?" asked Dorothy.

"Because if you did not wear spectacles the brightness and glory of the Emerald City would blind you. Even those who live in the City must wear spectacles night and day. They are all locked on, for Oz so ordered it when the City was first built, and I have the only key that will unlock them."

He opened the big box, and Dorothy saw that it was filled with spectacles of every size and shape. All of them had green glasses in them. The Guardian of the Gates found a pair that would just fit Dorothy and put them over her eyes. There were two golden bands fastened to them that passed around the back of her head, where they were locked together by a little key that was at the end of a chain the Guardian of the Gates wore around his neck. When they were on, Dorothy could not take them off had she wished, but of course she did not want to be blinded by the glare of the Emerald City, so she said nothing.

Then the green man fitted spectacles for the Scarecrow and the Tin Woodman and the Lion, and even on little Toto; and all were locked fast with the key.

Then the Guardian of the Gates put on his own glasses and told them he was ready to show them to the palace. Taking a big golden key from a peg on the wall he opened another gate, and they all followed him through the portal into the streets of the Emerald City.

" The Eyes looked at her thoughtfully."

CHAPTER XI

THE WONDERFUL EMERALD CITY OF OZ

E VEN WITH eyes protected by the green spectacles Dorothy and her friends were at first dazzled by the brilliancy of the wonderful City. The streets were lined with beautiful houses all built of green marble and studded everywhere with sparkling emeralds. They walked over a pavement of the same green marble, and where the blocks were joined together were rows of emeralds, set closely, and glittering in the brightness of the sun. The window panes were of green glass; even the sky above the City had a green tint, and the rays of the sun were green.

There were many people, men, women and children, walking about, and these were all dressed in green clothes and had greenish skins. They looked at Dorothy and her strangely assorted company with wondering eyes, and the children all ran away and hid behind their mothers when they saw the Lion; but no one spoke to them. Many shops stood in the street, and Dorothy saw that everything in them was green. Green candy and green pop-corn were offered for sale, as well as green shoes, green hats and green clothes of all sorts. At one place a man was selling green lemonade, and when the children bought it Dorothy could see that they paid for it with green pennies.

There seemed to be no horses nor animals of any kind; the men carried things around in little green carts, which they pushed before them. Everyone seemed happy and contented and prosperous.

The Guardian of the Gates led them through the streets until they came to a big building, exactly in the middle of the City, which was the Palace of Oz, the Great Wizard. There was a soldier before the door, dressed in a green uniform and wearing a long green beard.

"Here are strangers," said the Guardian of the Gates to him, "and they demand to see the Great Oz."

"Step inside," answered the soldier, "and I will carry your message to him."

So they passed through the Palace gates and were led into a big room with a green carpet and lovely green furniture set with emeralds. The soldier made them all wipe their feet upon a green mat before entering this room, and when they were seated he said, politely,

"Please make yourselves comfortable while I go to the door of the Throne Room and tell Oz you are here."

They had to wait a long time before the soldier returned. When, at last, he came back, Dorothy asked,

"Have you seen Oz?"

"Oh, no;" returned the soldier; "I have never seen him. But I spoke to him as he sat behind his screen, and gave him your message. He says he will grant you an audience, if you so desire; but each one of you must enter his presence alone, and he will admit but one each day. Therefore, as you must remain in the Palace for several days, I will have you shown to rooms where you may rest in comfort after your journey."

"Thank you," replied the girl; "that is very kind of Oz."

The soldier now blew upon a green whistle, and at once a young girl, dressed in a pretty green silk gown, entered the room. She had lovely green hair and green eyes, and she bowed low before Dorothy as she said,

"Follow me and I will show you your room."

So Dorothy said good-bye to all her friends except Toto, and taking the dog in her arms followed the green girl through seven passages and up three flights of stairs until they came to a room at the front of the Palace. It was the sweetest little room in the world, with a soft, comfortable bed that had sheets of green silk and a green velvet counterpane. There was a tiny fountain in the middle of the room, that shot a spray of green perfume into the air, to fall back into a beautifully carved green marble basin. Beautiful green flowers stood in the windows, and there was a shelf with a row of little green books. When Dorothy had time to open these books she found them full of queer green pictures that made her laugh, they were so funny.

In a wardrobe were many green dresses, made of silk

and satin and velvet; and all of them fitted Dorothy exactly.

"Make yourself perfectly at home," said the green girl, "and if you wish for anything ring the bell. Oz will send for you tomorrow morning."

She left Dorothy alone and went back to the others. These she also led to rooms, and each one of them found himself lodged in a very pleasant part of the Palace. Of course this politeness was wasted on the Scarecrow; for when he found himself alone in his room he stood stupidly in one spot, just within the doorway, to wait till morning. It would not rest him to lie down, and he could not close his eyes; so he remained all night staring at a little spider which was weaving its web in a corner of the room, just as if it were not one of the most wonderful rooms in the world. The Tin Woodman lay down on his bed from force of habit, for he remembered when he was made of flesh; but not being able to sleep he passed the night moving his joints up and down to make sure they kept in good working order. The Lion would have preferred a bed of dried leaves in the forest, and did not like being shut up in a room; but he had too much sense to let this worry him, so he sprang upon the bed and rolled himself up like a cat and purred himself asleep in a minute.

The next morning, after breakfast, the green maiden came to fetch Dorothy, and she dressed her in one of the prettiest gowns—made of green brocaded satin. Dorothy put on a green silk apron and tied a green ribbon around Toto's neck, and they started for the Throne Room of the Great Oz.

First they came to a great hall in which were many ladies and gentlemen of the court, all dressed in rich costumes. These people had nothing to do but talk to each other, but they always came to wait outside the Throne Room every morning, although they were never permitted to see Oz. As Dorothy entered they looked at her curiously, and one of them whispered,

"Are you really going to look upon the face of Oz the Terrible?"

"Of course," answered the girl, "if he will see me."

"Oh, he will see you," said the soldier who had taken her message to the Wizard, "although he does not like to have people ask to see him. Indeed, at first he was angry, and said I should send you back where you came from. Then he asked me what you looked like, and when I mentioned your silver shoes he was very much interested. At last I told him about the mark upon your forehead, and he decided he would admit you to his presence."

Just then a bell rang, and the green girl said to Dorothy,

"That is the signal. You must go into the Throne Room alone."

She opened a little door and Dorothy walked boldly through and found herself in a wonderful place. It was a big, round room with a high arched roof, and the walls and ceiling and floor were covered with large emeralds set closely together. In the center of the roof was a great light, as bright as the sun, which made the emeralds sparkle in a wonderful manner.

But what interested Dorothy most was the big throne of green marble that stood in the middle of the room. It was shaped like a chair and sparkled with gems, as did every-thing else. In the center of the chair was an enormous Head, without body to support it or any arms or legs whatever. There was no hair upon this head, but it had eyes and nose and mouth, and was bigger than the head of the biggest giant.

As Dorothy gazed upon this in wonder and fear the eyes turned slowly and looked at her sharply and steadily. Then the mouth moved, and Dorothy heard a voice say:

"I am Oz, the Great and Terrible. Who are you, and why do you seek me?"

It was not such an awful voice as she had expected to come from the big Head; so she took courage and answered,

"I am Dorothy, the Small and Meek. I have come to you for help."

The eyes looked at her thoughtfully for a full minute. Then said the voice:

"Where did you get the silver shoes?"

"I got them from the wicked Witch of the East, when my house fell on her and killed her," she replied.

"Where did you get the mark upon your forehead?" con-tinued the voice.

"That is where the good Witch of the North kissed me when she bade me good-bye and sent me to you," said the girl.

Again the eyes looked at her sharply, and they saw she was telling the truth. Then Oz asked,

"What do you wish me to do?"

"Send me back to Kansas, where my Aunt Em and Uncle

Henry are," she answered, earnestly. "I don't like your country, although it is so beautiful. And I am sure Aunt Em will be dreadfully worried over my being away so long."

The eyes winked three times, and then they turned up to the ceiling and down to the floor and rolled around so queerly that they seemed to see every part of the room. And at last they looked at Dorothy again.

"Why should I do this for you?" asked Oz.

"Because you are strong and I am weak; because you are a Great Wizard and I am only a helpless little girl," she answered.

"But you were strong enough to kill the wicked Witch of the East," said Oz.

"That just happened," returned Dorothy, simply; "I could not help it."

"Well," said the Head, "I will give you my answer. You have no right to expect me to send you back to Kansas unless you do something for me in return. In this country everyone must pay for everything he gets. If you wish me to use my magic power to send you home again you must do something for me first. Help me and I will help you."

"What must I do?" asked the girl.

"Kill the wicked Witch of the West," answered Oz.

"But I cannot!" exclaimed Dorothy, greatly surprised.

"You killed the Witch of the East and you wear the silver shoes, which bear a powerful charm. There is now but one Wicked Witch left in all this land, and when you can tell me she is dead I will send you back to Kansas—but not before."

The little girl began to weep, she was so much disappointed; and the eyes winked again and looked upon her anxiously, as if the Great Oz felt that she could help him if she would.

"I never killed anything, willingly," she sobbed; "and even if I wanted to, how could I kill the Wicked Witch? If you, who are Great and Terrible, cannot kill her yourself, how do you expect me to do it?"

"I do not know," said the Head; "but that is my answer, and until the Wicked Witch dies you will not see your Uncle and Aunt again. Remember that the Witch is Wicked—tremendously Wicked—and ought to be killed. Now go, and do not ask to see me again until you have done your task."

Sorrowfully Dorothy left the Throne Room and went back where the Lion and the Scarecrow and the Tin Woodman were waiting to hear what Oz had said to her.

"There is no hope for me," she said, sadly, "for Oz will not send me home until I have killed the Wicked Witch of the West; and that I can never do."

Her friends were sorry, but could do nothing to help her; so she went to her own room and lay down on the bed and cried herself to sleep.

The next morning the soldier with the green whiskers came to the Scarecrow and said,

"Come with me, for Oz has sent for you."

So the Scarecrow followed him and was admitted into the great Throne Room, where he saw, sitting in the emerald throne, a most lovely lady. She was dressed in green silk gauze and wore upon her flowing green locks a crown of jewels. Growing from her shoulders were wings, gorgeous in color and so light that they fluttered if the slightest breath of air reached them.

When the Scarecrow had bowed, as prettily as his straw stuffing would let him, before this beautiful creature, she looked upon him sweetly, and said,

"I am Oz, the Great and Terrible. Who are you, and why do you seek me?"

Now the Scarecrow, who had expected to see the great Head Dorothy had told him of, was much astonished; but he answered her bravely:

"I am only a Scarecrow, stuffed with straw. Therefore I have no brains, and I come to you praying that you will put brains in my head instead of straw, so that I may become as much a man as any other in your dominions."

"Why should I do this for you?" asked the lady.

"Because you are wise and powerful, and no one else can help me," answered the Scarecrow.

"I never grant favors without some return," said Oz; "but this much I will promise. If you will kill for me the Wicked Witch of the West I will bestow upon you a great many brains, and such good brains that you will be the wisest man in all the Land of Oz."

"I thought you asked Dorothy to kill the Witch," said the Scarecrow, in surprise.

"So I did. I don't care who kills her. But until she is dead I will not grant your wish. Now go, and do not seek me again until you have earned the brains you so greatly desire."

The Scarecrow went sorrowfully back to his friends and told them what Oz had said; and Dorothy was surprised to find that the great Wizard was not a Head, as she had seen him, but a lovely lady.

"All the same," said the Scarecrow, "she needs a heart as much as the Tin Woodman."

On the next morning the soldier with the green whiskers came to the Tin Woodman and said,

"Oz has sent for you. Follow me."

So the Tin Woodman followed him and came to the great Throne Room. He did not know whether he would find Oz a lovely lady or a Head, but he hoped it would be the lovely lady. "For," he said to himself, "if it is the Head, I am sure I shall not be given a heart, since a head has no heart of its own and therefore cannot feel for me. But if it is the lovely lady I shall beg hard for a heart, for all ladies are themselves said to be kindly hearted."

But when the Woodman entered the great Throne Room he saw neither the Head nor the Lady, for Oz had taken the shape of a most terrible Beast. It was nearly as big as an elephant, and the green throne seemed hardly strong enough to hold its weight. The Beast had a head like that of a rhinoceros, only there were five eyes in its face. There were five long arms growing out of its body and it also had five long, slim legs. Thick, woolly hair covered every part of it, and a more dreadful looking monster could not be imagined. It was fortunate the Tin Woodman had no heart at that moment, for it would have beat loud and fast from terror. But being only tin, the Woodman was not at all afraid, although he was much disappointed.

"I am Oz, the Great and Terrible," spake the Beast, in a voice that was one great roar. "Who are you, and why do you seek me?"

"I am a Woodman, and made of tin. Therefore I have no heart, and cannot love. I pray you to give me a heart that I may be as other men are."

"Why should I do this?" demanded the Beast.

"Because I ask it, and you alone can grant my request," answered the Woodman.

Oz gave a low growl at this, but said, gruffly,

"If you indeed desire a heart, you must earn it."

"How?" asked the Woodman.

"Help Dorothy to kill the Wicked Witch of the West," replied the Beast. "When the Witch is dead, come to me, and I will then give you the biggest and kindest and most loving heart in all the Land of Oz."

So the Tin Woodman was forced to return sorrowfully to his friends and tell them of the terrible Beast he had seen. They all wondered greatly at the many forms the great Wizard could take upon himself, and the Lion said,

"If he is a beast when I go to see him, I shall roar my loudest, and so frighten him that he will grant all I ask. And if he is the lovely lady, I shall pretend to spring upon her, and so compel her to do my bidding. And if he is the great Head, he will be at my mercy; for I will roll this head all about the room until he promises to give us what we desire. So be of good cheer my friends, for all will yet be well."

The next morning the soldier with the green whiskers led the Lion to the great Throne Room and bade him enter the presence of Oz.

The Lion at once passed through the door, and glancing around saw, to his surprise, that before the throne was a Ball of Fire, so fierce and glowing he could scarcely bear to gaze upon it. His first thought was that Oz had by accident caught on fire and was burning up; but, when he tried to go nearer, the heat was so intense that it singed his whiskers, and he crept back tremblingly to a spot nearer the door.

Then a low, quiet voice came from the Ball of Fire, and these were the words it spoke:

"I am Oz, the Great and Terrible. Who are you, and why do you seek me?"

And the Lion answered,

"I am a Cowardly Lion, afraid of everything. I come to you to beg that you give me courage, so that in reality I may become the King of Beasts, as men call me."

"Why should I give you courage?" demanded Oz.

"Because of all Wizards you are the greatest, and alone have power to grant my request," answered the Lion.

The Ball of Fire burned fiercely for a time, and the voice said,

"Bring me proof that the Wicked Witch is dead, and that moment I will give you courage. But so long as the Witch lives you must remain a coward."

The Lion was angry at this speech, but could say nothing in reply, and while he stood silently gazing at the Ball of Fire it became so furiously hot that he turned tail and rushed from the room. He was glad to find his friends waiting for him, and told them of his terrible interview with the Wizard.

"What shall we do now?" asked Dorothy, sadly.

"There is only one thing we can do," returned the Lion, "and that is to go to the land of the Winkies, seek out the Wicked Witch, and destroy her."

"But suppose we cannot?" said the girl.

"Then I shall never have courage," declared the Lion.

"And I shall never have brains," added the Scarecrow.

"And I shall never have a heart," spoke the Tin Woodman.

"And I shall never see Aunt Em and Uncle Henry," said Dorothy, beginning to cry.

"Be careful!" cried the green girl, "the tears will fall on your green silk gown, and spot it."

So Dorothy dried her eyes and said,

"I suppose we must try it; but I am sure I do not want to kill anybody, even to see Aunt Em again."

"I will go with you; but I'm too much of a coward to kill the Witch," said the Lion.

"I will go too," declared the Scarecrow; "but I shall not be of much help to you, I am such a fool."

"I haven't the heart to harm even a Witch," remarked the Tin Woodman; "but if you go I certainly shall go with you."

Therefore it was decided to start upon their journey the next morning, and the Woodman sharpened his axe on a green grindstone and had all his joints properly oiled. The Scarecrow stuffed himself with fresh straw and Dorothy put new paint on his eyes that he might see better. The green girl, who was very kind to them, filled Dorothy's basket with good things to eat, and fastened a little bell around Toto's neck with a green ribbon.

They went to bed quite early and slept soundly until daylight, when they were awakened by the crowing of a green cock that lived in the back yard of the palace, and the cackling of a hen that had laid a green egg.

" The Soldier with the green whiskers led them through the streets."

" The Monkeys wound many coils about his body."

CHAPTER XII

THE SEARCH FOR THE WICKED WITCH

THE SOLDIER with the green whiskers led them through the streets of the Emerald City until they reached the room where the Guardian of the Gates lived. This officer unlocked their spectacles to put them back in his great box, and then he politely opened the gate for our friends.

"Which road leads to the Wicked Witch of the West?" asked Dorothy.

"There is no road," answered the Guardian of the Gates; "no one ever wishes to go that way."

"How, then, are we to find her?" enquired the girl.

"That will be easy," replied the man; "for when she knows you are in the Country of the Winkies she will find you, and make you all her slaves."

"Perhaps not," said the Scarecrow, "for we mean to destroy her."

"Oh, that is different," said the Guardian of the Gates. "No one has ever destroyed her before, so I naturally thought she would make slaves of you, as she has of all the rest. But take care; for she is wicked and fierce, and may not allow you to destroy her. Keep to the West, where the sun sets, and you cannot fail to find her."

They thanked him and bade him good-bye, and turned toward the West, walking over fields of soft grass dotted here and there with daisies and buttercups. Dorothy still wore the pretty silk dress she had put on in the palace, but now, to her surprise, she found it was no longer green, but pure white. The ribbon around Toto's neck had also lost its green color and was as white as Dorothy's dress.

The Emerald City was soon left far behind. As they advanced the ground became rougher and hillier, for there were no farms nor houses in this country of the West, and the ground was untilled.

In the afternoon the sun shone hot in their faces, for there were no trees to offer them shade; so that before night Dorothy and Toto and the Lion were tired, and lay down upon the grass and fell asleep, with the Woodman and the Scarecrow keeping watch.

Now the Wicked Witch of the West had but one eye, yet that was as powerful as a telescope, and could see everywhere. So, as she sat in the door of her castle, she happened to look around and saw Dorothy lying asleep, with her friends all about her. They were a long distance off, but the

Wicked Witch was angry to find them in her country; so she blew upon a silver whistle that hung around her neck.

At once there came running to her from all directions a pack of great wolves. They had long legs and fierce eyes and sharp teeth.

"Go to those people," said the Witch, "and tear them to pieces."

"Are you not going to make them your slaves?" asked the leader of the wolves.

"No," she answered, "one is of tin, and one of straw; one is a girl and another a Lion. None of them is fit to work, so you may tear them into small pieces."

"Very well," said the wolf, and he dashed away at full speed, followed by the others.

It was lucky the Scarecrow and the Woodman were wide awake and heard the wolves coming.

"This is my fight," said the Woodman; "so get behind me and I will meet them as they come."

He seized his axe, which he had made very sharp, and as the leader of the wolves came on the Tin Woodman swung his arm and chopped the wolf's head from its body, so that it immediately died. As soon as he could raise his axe another wolf came up, and he also fell under the sharp edge of the Tin Woodman's weapon. There were forty wolves, and forty times a wolf was killed; so that at last they all lay dead in a heap before the Woodman.

Then he put down his axe and sat beside the Scarecrow, who said,

"It was a good fight, friend."

They waited until Dorothy awoke the next morning. The little girl was quite frightened when she saw the great pile of shaggy wolves, but the Tin Woodman told her all. She thanked him for saving them and sat down to breakfast, after which they started again upon their journey.

Now this same morning the Wicked Witch came to the door of her castle and looked out with her one eye that could see afar off. She saw all her wolves lying dead, and the strangers still travelling through her country. This made her angrier than before, and she blew her silver whistle twice.

Straightway a great flock of wild crows came flying toward her, enough to darken the sky. And the Wicked Witch said to the King Crow,

"Fly at once to the strangers; peck out their eyes and tear them to pieces."

The wild crows flew in one great flock toward Dorothy and her companions. When the little girl saw them coming she was afraid. But the Scarecrow said,

"This is my battle; so lie down beside me and you will not be harmed."

So they all lay upon the ground except the Scarecrow, and he stood up and stretched out his arms. And when the crows saw him they were frightened, as these birds always are by scarecrows, and did not dare to come any nearer. But the King Crow said,

"It is only a stuffed man. I will peck his eyes out."

The King Crow flew at the Scarecrow, who caught it by the head and twisted its neck until it died. And then another crow flew at him, and the Scarecrow twisted its neck also.

There were forty crows, and forty times the Scarecrow twisted a neck, until at last all were lying dead beside him. Then he called to his companions to rise, and again they went upon their journey.

When the Wicked Witch looked out again and saw all her crows lying in a heap, she got into a terrible rage, and blew three times upon her silver whistle.

Forthwith there was heard a great buzzing in the air, and a swarm of black bees came flying towards her.

"Go to the strangers and sting them to death!" commanded the Witch, and the bees turned and flew rapidly until they came to where Dorothy and her friends were walking. But the Woodman had seen them coming and the Scarecrow had decided what to do.

"Take out my straw and scatter it over the little girl and the dog and the lion," he said to the Woodman, "and the bees cannot sting them." This the Woodman did, and as Dorothy lay close beside the Lion and held Toto in her arms, the straw covered them entirely.

The bees came and found no one but the Woodman to sting, so they flew at him and broke off all their stings against the tin, without hurting the Woodman at all. And as bees cannot live when their stings are broken that was the end of the black bees, and they lay scattered thick about the Woodman, like little heaps of fine coal.

Then Dorothy and the Lion got up, and the girl helped the Tin Woodman put the straw back into the Scarecrow again, until he was as good as ever. So they started upon their journey once more.

The Wicked Witch was so angry when she saw her black

bees in little heaps like fine coal that she stamped her foot and tore her hair and gnashed her teeth. And then she called a dozen of her slaves, who were the Winkies, and gave them sharp spears, telling them to go to the strangers and destroy them.

The Winkies were not a brave people, but they had to do as they were told; so they marched away until they came near to Dorothy. Then the Lion gave a great roar and sprang toward them, and the poor Winkies were so frightened that they ran back as fast as they could.

When they returned to the castle the Wicked Witch beat them well with a strap, and sent them back to their work, after which she sat down to think what she should do next. She could not understand how all her plans to destroy these strangers had failed; but she was a powerful Witch, as well as a wicked one, and she soon made up her mind how to act.

There was, in her cupboard, a Golden Cap, with a circle of diamonds and rubies running round it. This Golden Cap had a charm. Whoever owned it could call three times upon the Winged Monkeys, who would obey any order they were given. But no person could command these strange creatures more than three times. Twice already the Wicked Witch had used the charm of the Cap. Once was when she had made the Winkies her slaves, and set herself to rule over their country. The Winged Monkeys had helped her do this. The second time was when she had fought against the Great Oz himself, and driven him out of the land of the West. The Winged Monkeys had also helped her in doing this. Only once more could she use this Golden Cap, for which reason she did not like to do so until all her other powers were exhausted. But now that her fierce wolves and her wild crows and her stinging bees were gone, and her slaves had been scared away by the Cowardly Lion, she saw there was only one way left to destroy Dorothy and her friends.

So the Wicked Witch took the Golden Cap from her cupboard and placed it upon her head. Then she stood upon her left foot and said, slowly,

"Ep-pe, pep-pe, kak-ke!"

Next she stood upon her right foot and said,

"Hil-lo, hol-lo, hel-lo!"

After this she stood upon both feet and cried in a loud voice,

"Ziz-zy, zuz-zy, zik!"

Now the charm began to work. The sky was darkened, and a low rumbling sound was heard in the air. There was a rushing of many wings; a great chattering and laughing; and the sun came out of the dark sky to show the Wicked Witch surrounded by a crowd of monkeys, each with a pair of immense and powerful wings on his shoulders.

One, much bigger than the others, seemed to be their leader. He flew close to the Witch and said,

"You have called us for the third and last time. What do you command?"

"Go to the strangers who are within my land and destroy them all except the Lion," said the Wicked Witch. "Bring that beast to me, for I have a mind to harness him like a horse, and make him work."

"Your commands shall be obeyed," said the leader; and

then, with a great deal of chattering and noise, the Winged Monkeys flew away to the place where Dorothy and her friends were walking.

Some of the Monkeys seized the Tin Woodman and carried him through the air until they were over a country thickly covered with sharp rocks. Here they dropped the poor Woodman, who fell a great distance to the rocks, where he lay so battered and dented that he could neither move nor groan.

Others of the Monkeys caught the Scarecrow, and with their long fingers pulled all of the straw out of his clothes and head. They made his hat and boots and clothes into a small bundle and threw it into the top branches of a tall tree.

The remaining Monkeys threw pieces of stout rope around the Lion and wound many coils about his body and head and legs, until he was unable to bite or scratch or struggle in any way. Then they lifted him up and flew away with him to the Witch's castle, where he was placed in a small yard with a high iron fence around it, so that he could not escape.

But Dorothy they did not harm at all. She stood, with Toto in her arms, watching the sad fate of her comrades and thinking it would soon be her turn. The leader of the Winged Monkeys flew up to her, his long, hairy arms stretched out and his ugly face grinning terribly; but he saw the mark of the Good Witch's kiss upon her forehead and stopped short, motioning the others not to touch her.

"We dare not harm this little girl," he said to them, "for she is protected by the Power of Good, and that is greater than the Power of Evil. All we can do is to carry her to the castle of the Wicked Witch and leave her there."

So, carefully and gently, they lifted Dorothy in their arms and carried her swiftly through the air until they came to the castle, where they set her down upon the front door step. Then the leader said to the Witch,

"We have obeyed you as far as we were able. The Tin Woodman and the Scarecrow are destroyed, and the Lion is tied up in your yard. The little girl we dare not harm, nor the dog she carries in her arms. Your power over our band is now ended, and you will never see us again."

Then all the Winged Monkeys, with much laughing and chattering and noise, flew into the air and were soon out of sight.

The Wicked Witch was both surprised and worried when she saw the mark on Dorothy's forehead, for she knew well that neither the Winged Monkeys nor she, herself, dare hurt the girl in any way. She looked down at Dorothy's feet, and seeing the Silver Shoes, began to tremble with fear, for she knew what a powerful charm belonged to them. At first the Witch was tempted to run away from Dorothy; but she hap- pened to look into the child's eyes and saw how simple the soul behind them was, and that the little girl did not know of the wonderful power the Silver Shoes gave her. So the Wicked Witch laughed to herself, and thought, "I can still make her my slave, for she does not know how to use her power." Then she said to Dorothy, harshly and severely,

"Come with me; and see that you mind everything I tell you, for if you do not I will make an end of you, as I did of the Tin Woodman and the Scarecrow."

Dorothy followed her through many of the beautiful rooms in her castle until they came to the kitchen, where the Witch bade her clean the pots and kettles and sweep the floor and keep the fire fed with wood.

Dorothy went to work meekly, with her mind made up to work as hard as she could; for she was glad the Wicked Witch had decided not to kill her.

With Dorothy hard at work the Witch thought she would go into the court-yard and harness the Cowardly Lion like a horse; it would amuse her, she was sure, to make him draw her chariot whenever she wished to go to drive. But as she opened the gate the Lion gave a loud roar and bounded at her so fiercely that the Witch was afraid, and ran out and shut the gate again.

"If I cannot harness you," said the Witch to the Lion, speaking through the bars of the gate, "I can starve you. You shall have nothing to eat until you do as I wish."

So after that she took no food to the imprisoned Lion; but every day she came to the gate at noon and asked,

"Are you ready to be harnessed like a horse?"

And the Lion would answer,

"No. If you come in this yard I will bite you."

The reason the Lion did not have to do as the Witch wished was that every night, while the woman was asleep, Dorothy carried him food from the cupboard. After he had eaten he would lie down on his bed of straw, and Dorothy would lie beside him and put her head on his soft, shaggy mane, while they talked of their troubles and tried to plan some way to escape. But they could find no way to get out of the castle, for it was constantly guarded by the yellow

Winkies, who were the slaves of the Wicked Witch and too afraid of her not to do as she told them.

The girl had to work hard during the day, and often the Witch threatened to beat her with the same old umbrella she always carried in her hand. But, in truth, she did not dare to strike Dorothy, because of the mark upon her forehead. The child did not know this, and was full of fear for herself and Toto. Once the Witch struck Toto a blow with her umbrella and the brave little dog flew at her and bit her leg, in return. The Witch did not bleed where she was bitten, for she was so wicked that the blood in her had dried up many years before.

Dorothy's life became very sad as she grew to understand that it would be harder than ever to get back to Kansas and Aunt Em again. Sometimes she would cry bitterly for hours, with Toto sitting at her feet and looking into her face, whining dismally to show how sorry he was for his little mistress. Toto did not really care whether he was in Kansas or the Land of Oz so long as Dorothy was with him; but he knew the little girl was unhappy, and that made him unhappy too.

Now the Wicked Witch had a great longing to have for her own the Silver Shoes which the girl always wore. Her Bees and her Crows and her Wolves were lying in heaps and drying up, and she had used up all the power of the Golden Cap; but if she could only get hold of the Silver Shoes they would give her more power than all the other things she had lost. She watched Dorothy carefully, to see if she ever took off her shoes, thinking she might steal them. But the child was so proud of her pretty shoes that she never took them off except at night and when she took her bath. The Witch was too much afraid of the dark to dare go in Dorothy's room at night to take the shoes, and her dread of water was greater than her fear of the dark, so she never came near when Dorothy was bathing. Indeed, the old Witch never touched water, nor ever let water touch her in any way.

But the wicked creature was very cunning, and she finally thought of a trick that would give her what she wanted. She placed a bar of iron in the middle of the kitchen floor, and then by her magic arts made the iron invisible to human eyes. So that when Dorothy walked across the floor she stumbled over the bar, not being able to see it, and fell at full length. She was not much hurt, but in her fall one of the Silver Shoes came off, and before she could reach it the Witch had snatched it away and put it on her own skinny foot.

The wicked woman was greatly pleased with the success of her trick, for as long as she had one of the shoes she owned half the power of their charm, and Dorothy could not use it against her, even had she known how to do so.

The little girl, seeing she had lost one of her pretty shoes, grew angry, and said to the Witch,

"Give me back my shoe!"

"I will not," retorted the Witch, "for it is now my shoe, and not yours."

"You are a wicked creature!" cried Dorothy. "You have no right to take my shoe from me."

"I shall keep it, just the same," said the Witch, laughing at her, "and some day I shall get the other one from you, too."

This made Dorothy so very angry that she picked up the bucket of water that stood near and dashed it over the Witch, wetting her from head to foot.

Instantly the wicked woman gave a loud cry of fear; and then, as Dorothy looked at her in wonder, the Witch began to shrink and fall away.

"See what you have done!" she screamed. "In a minute I shall melt away."

"I'm very sorry, indeed," said Dorothy, who was truly frightened to see the Witch actually melting away like brown sugar before her very eyes.

"Didn't you know water would be the end of me?" asked the Witch, in a wailing, despairing voice.

"Of course not," answered Dorothy; "how should I?"

"Well, in a few minutes I shall be all melted, and you will have the castle to yourself. I have been wicked in my day, but I never thought a little girl like you would ever be able to melt me and end my wicked deeds. Look out—here I go!"

With these words the Witch fell down in a brown, melted, shapeless mass and began to spread over the clean boards of the kitchen floor. Seeing that she had really melted away to nothing, Dorothy drew another bucket of water and threw it over the mess. She then swept it all out the door. After picking out the silver shoe, which was all that was left of the old woman, she cleaned and dried it with a cloth, and put it on her foot again. Then, being at last free to do as she chose, she ran out to the court-yard to tell the Lion that the Wicked Witch of the West had come to an end, and that they were no longer prisoners in a strange land.

"*The Tinsmiths worked for three days and four nights.*"

CHAPTER XIII

THE RESCUE

THE COWARDLY Lion was much pleased to hear that the Wicked Witch had been melted by a bucket of water, and Dorothy at once unlocked the gate of his prison and set him free. They went in together to the castle, where Dorothy's first act was to call all the Winkies together and tell them that they were no longer slaves.

There was great rejoicing among the yellow Winkies, for they had been made to work hard during many years for the Wicked Witch, who had always treated them with great cruelty. They kept this day as a holiday, then and ever after, and spent the time in feasting and dancing.

"If our friends, the Scarecrow and the Tin Woodman, were only with us," said the Lion, "I should be quite happy."

"Don't you suppose we could rescue them?" asked the girl, anxiously.

"We can try," answered the Lion.

So they called the yellow Winkies and asked them if they would help to rescue their friends, and the Winkies said that they would be delighted to do all in their power for Dorothy, who had set them free from bondage. So she chose a number of the Winkies who looked as if they knew the most, and they all started away. They travelled that day and part of the next until they came to the rocky plain where the Tin Woodman lay, all battered and bent. His axe was near him, but the blade was rusted and the handle broken off short.

The Winkies lifted him tenderly in their arms, and carried him back to the yellow castle again, Dorothy shedding a few tears by the way at the sad plight of her old friend, and the Lion looking sober and sorry. When they reached the castle Dorothy said to the Winkies,

"Are any of your people tinsmiths?"

"Oh, yes; some of us are very good tinsmiths," they told her.

"Then bring them to me," she said. And when the tinsmiths came, bringing with them all their tools in baskets, she enquired,

"Can you straighten out those dents in the Tin Woodman, and bend him back into shape again, and solder him together where he is broken?"

The tinsmiths looked the Woodman over carefully and then answered that they thought they could mend him so he would be as good as ever. So they set to work in one of the big yellow rooms of the castle and worked for three days and four nights, hammering and twisting and bending and soldering and polishing and pounding at the legs and body and head of the Tin Woodman, until at last he was straightened out into his old form, and his joints worked as well as ever. To be sure, there were several patches on him, but the tinsmiths did a good job, and as the Woodman was not a vain man he did not mind the patches at all.

When, at last, he walked into Dorothy's room and thanked her for rescuing him, he was so pleased that he wept tears of joy, and Dorothy had to wipe every tear carefully from his face with her apron, so his joints would not be rusted. At the same time her own tears fell thick and fast at the joy of meeting her old friend again, and these tears did not need to be wiped away. As for the Lion, he wiped his eyes so often with the tip of his tail that it became quite wet, and he was obliged to go out into the court-yard and hold it in the sun till it dried.

"If we only had the Scarecrow with us again," said the Tin Woodman, when Dorothy had finished telling him everything that had happened, "I should be quite happy."

"We must try to find him," said the girl.

So she called the Winkies to help her, and they walked all that day and part of the next until they came to the tall tree in the branches of which the Winged Monkeys had tossed the Scarecrow's clothes.

It was a very tall tree, and the trunk was so smooth that no one could climb it; but the Woodman said at once,

"I'll chop it down, and then we can get the Scarecrow's clothes."

Now while the tinsmiths had been at work mending the Woodman himself, another of the Winkies, who was a goldsmith, had made an axe-handle of solid gold and fitted it to the Woodman's axe, instead of the old broken handle. Others polished the blade until all the rust was removed and it glistened like burnished silver.

As soon as he had spoken, the Tin Woodman began to chop, and in a short time the tree fell over with a crash, when the Scarecrow's clothes fell out of the branches and rolled off on the ground.

Dorothy picked them up and had the Winkies carry them back to the castle, where they were stuffed with nice, clean straw; and, behold! here was the Scarecrow, as good as ever, thanking them over and over again for saving him.

Now they were reunited, Dorothy and her friends spent a few happy days at the Yellow Castle, where they found everything they needed to make them comfortable. But one day the girl thought of Aunt Em, and said,

"We must go back to Oz, and claim his promise."

"Yes," said the Woodman, "at last I shall get my heart."

"And I shall get my brains," added the Scarecrow, joyfully.

"And I shall get my courage," said the Lion, thoughtfully.

"And I shall get back to Kansas," cried Dorothy, clapping her hands. "Oh, let us start for the Emerald City to-morrow!"

This they decided to do. The next day they called the Winkies together and bade them good-bye. The Winkies were sorry to have them go, and they had grown so fond of the Tin Woodman that they begged him to stay and rule over them and the Yellow Land of the West. Finding they were determined to go, the Winkies gave Toto and the Lion each a golden collar; and to Dorothy they presented a beautiful bracelet, studded with diamonds; and to the Scarecrow they gave a gold-headed walking stick, to keep him from stumbling; and to the Tin Woodman they offered a silver oil-can, inlaid with gold and set with precious jewels.

Every one of the travellers made the Winkies a pretty speech in return, and all shook hands with them until their arms ached.

Dorothy went to the Witch's cupboard to fill her basket with food for the journey, and there she saw the Golden Cap. She tried it on her own head and found that it fitted her exactly. She did not know anything about the charm of the Golden Cap, but she saw that it was pretty, so she made up her mind to wear it and carry her sunbonnet in the basket.

Then, being prepared for the journey, they all started for the Emerald City; and the Winkies gave them three cheers and many good wishes to carry with them.

" The Monkeys caught Dorothy in their arms and flew away with her."

CHAPTER XIV

THE WINGED MONKEYS

YOU WILL remember there was no road—not even a pathway—between the castle of the Wicked Witch and the Emerald City. When the four travellers went in search of the Witch she had seen them coming, and so sent the Winged Monkeys to bring them to her. It was much harder to find their way back through the big fields of buttercups and yellow daisies than it was being carried. They knew, of course, they must go straight east, toward the rising sun; and they started off in the right way. But at noon, when the sun was over their heads, they did not know which was east and which was west, and that was the reason they were lost in the great fields. They kept on walking, however, and at night the moon came out and shone brightly. So they lay down among the sweet smelling yellow flowers and slept soundly until morning—all but the Scarecrow and the Tin Woodman.

The next morning the sun was behind a cloud, but they started on, as if they were quite sure which way they were going.

"If we walk far enough," said Dorothy, "we shall sometime come to some place, I am sure."

But day by day passed away, and they still saw nothing before them but the yellow fields. The Scarecrow began to grumble a bit.

"We have surely lost our way," he said, "and unless we find it again in time to reach the Emerald City I shall never get my brains."

"Nor I my heart," declared the Tin Woodman. "It seems to me I can scarcely wait till I get to Oz, and you must admit this is a very long journey."

"You see," said the Cowardly Lion, with a whimper, "I haven't the courage to keep tramping forever, without getting anywhere at all."

Then Dorothy lost heart. She sat down on the grass and looked at her companions, and they sat down and looked at her, and Toto found that for the first time in his life he was too tired to chase a butterfly that flew past his head; so he put out his tongue and panted and looked at Dorothy as if to ask what they should do next.

"Suppose we call the Field Mice," she suggested. "They could probably tell us the way to the Emerald City."

"To be sure they could," cried the Scarecrow; "why didn't we think of that before?"

Dorothy blew the little whistle she had always carried

about her neck since the Queen of the Mice had given it to her. In a few minutes they heard the pattering of tiny feet, and many of the small grey mice came running up to her. Among them was the Queen herself, who asked, in her squeaky little voice,

"What can I do for my friends?"

"We have lost our way," said Dorothy. "Can you tell us where the Emerald City is?"

"Certainly," answered the Queen; "but it is a great way off, for you have had it at your backs all this time." Then she noticed Dorothy's Golden Cap, and said, "Why don't you use the charm of the Cap, and call the Winged Monkeys to you? They will carry you to the City of Oz in less than an hour."

"I didn't know there was a charm," answered Dorothy, in surprise. "What is it?"

"It is written inside the Golden Cap," replied the Queen of the Mice; "but if you are going to call the Winged Monkeys we must run away, for they are full of mischief and think it great fun to plague us."

"Won't they hurt me?" asked the girl, anxiously.

"Oh, no; they must obey the wearer of the Cap. Good-bye!" And she scampered out of sight, with all the mice hurrying after her.

Dorothy looked inside the Golden Cap and saw some words written upon the lining. These, she thought, must be the charm, so she read the directions carefully and put the Cap upon her head.

"Ep-pe, pep-pe, kak-ke!" she said, standing on her left foot.

"What did you say?" asked the Scarecrow, who did not know what she was doing.

"Hil-lo, hol-lo, hel-lo!" Dorothy went on, standing this time on her right foot.

"Hello!" replied the Tin Woodman, calmly.

"Ziz-zy, zuz-zy, zik!" said Dorothy, who was now standing on both feet. This ended the saying of the charm, and they heard a great chattering and flapping of wings, as the band of Winged Monkeys flew up to them. The King bowed low before Dorothy, and asked,

"What is your command?"

"We wish to go to the Emerald City," said the child, "and we have lost our way."

"We will carry you," replied the King, and no sooner had he spoken than than two of the Monkeys caught Dorothy in their arms and flew away with her. Others took the Scarecrow and the Woodman and the Lion, and one little Monkey seized Toto and flew after them, although the dog tried hard to bite him.

The Scarecrow and the Tin Woodman were rather frightened at first, for they remembered how badly the Winged Monkeys had treated them before; but they saw that no harm was intended, so they rode through the air quite cheerfully, and had a fine time looking at the pretty gardens and woods far below them.

Dorothy found herself riding easily between two of the biggest Monkeys, one of them the King himself. They had made a chair of their hands and were careful not to hurt her.

"Why do you have to obey the charm of the Golden Cap?" she asked.

"That is a long story," answered the King, with a laugh; "but as we have a long journey before us I will pass the time by telling you about it, if you wish."

"I shall be glad to hear it," she replied.

"Once," began the leader, "we were a free people, living happily in the great forest, flying from tree to tree, eating nuts and fruit, and doing just as we pleased without calling anybody master. Perhaps some of us were rather too full of mischief at times, flying down to pull the tails of the animals that had no wings, chasing birds, and throwing nuts at the people who walked in the forest. But we were careless and happy and full of fun, and enjoyed every minute of the day. This was many years ago, long before Oz came out of the clouds to rule over this land.

"There lived here then, away at the North, a beautiful princess, who was also a powerful sorceress. All her magic was used to help the people, and she was never known to hurt anyone who was good. Her name was Gayelette, and she lived in a handsome palace built from great blocks of ruby. Everyone loved her, but her greatest sorrow was that she could find no one to love in return, since all the men were much too stupid and ugly to mate with one so beautiful and wise. At last, however, she found a boy who was handsome and manly and wise beyond his years. Gayelette made up her mind that when he grew to be a man she would make him her husband, so she took him to her ruby palace and used all her magic powers to make him as strong and good and lovely as any woman could wish. When he grew to manhood, Quelala, as he was called, was said to be the best and wisest man in all the land, while his manly beauty was so great that Gayelette loved him dearly, and hastened to make everything ready for the wedding.

"My grandfather was at that time the King of the Winged Monkeys which lived in the forest near Gayelette's palace, and the old fellow loved a joke better than a good dinner. One day, just before the wedding, my grandfather was flying out with his band when he saw Quelala walking beside the river. He was dressed in a rich costume of pink silk and purple velvet, and my grandfather thought he would see what he could do. At his word the band flew down and seized Quelala, carried him in their arms until they were over the middle of the river, and then dropped him into the water.

" 'Swim out, my fine fellow,' cried my grandfather, 'and see if the water has spotted your clothes.' Quelala was much too wise not to swim, and he was not in the least spoiled by all his good fortune. He laughed, when he came to the top of the water, and swam in to shore. But when Gayelette came running out to him she found his silks and velvet all ruined by the river.

"The princess was very angry, and she knew, of course, who did it. She had all the Winged Monkeys brought before her, and she said at first that their wings should be tied and they should be treated as they had treated Quelala, and dropped in the river. But my grandfather pleaded hard, for he knew the Monkeys would drown in the river with their wings tied, and Quelala said a kind word for them also; so that Gayelette finally spared them, on condition that the Winged Monkeys should ever after do three times the bidding of the owner of the Golden Cap. This Cap had been made for a wedding present to Quelala, and it is said to have cost the princess half her kingdom. Of course my grandfather and all the other Monkeys at once agreed to the condition, and that is how it happens that we are three times the slaves of the owner of the Golden Cap, whomsoever he may be."

"And what became of them?" asked Dorothy, who had been greatly interested in the story.

"Quelala being the first owner of the Golden Cap," replied the Monkey, "he was the first to lay his wishes upon us. As his bride could not bear the sight of us, he called us all to him in the forest after he had married her and ordered us to always keep where she could never again set eyes on a Winged Monkey, which we were glad to do, for we were all afraid of her.

"This was all we ever had to do until the Golden Cap fell into the hands of the Wicked Witch of the West, who made us enslave the Winkies, and afterward drive Oz himself out of the Land of the West. Now the Golden Cap is yours, and three times you have the right to lay your wishes upon us."

As the Monkey King finished his story Dorothy looked down and saw the green, shining walls of the Emerald City before them. She wondered at the rapid flight of the Monkeys, but was glad the journey was over. The strange creatures set the travellers down carefully before the gate of the City, the King bowed low to Dorothy, and then flew swiftly away, followed by all his band.

"That was a good ride," said the little girl.

"Yes, and a quick way out of our troubles," replied the Lion. "How lucky it was you brought away that wonderful Cap!"

" Exactly so !   I am a humbug."

CHAPTER XV

THE DISCOVERY OF OZ, THE TERRIBLE

T HE FOUR travellers walked up to the great gate of the Emerald City and rang the bell. After ringing several times it was opened by the same Guardian of the Gates they had met before.

"What! are you back again?" he asked, in surprise.

"Do you not see us?" answered the Scarecrow.

"But I thought you had gone to visit the Wicked Witch of the West."

"We did visit her," said the Scarecrow.

"And she let you go again?" asked the man, in wonder.

"She could not help it, for she is melted," explained the Scarecrow.

"Melted! Well, that is good news, indeed," said the man. "Who melted her?"

"It was Dorothy," said the Lion, gravely.

"Good gracious!" exclaimed the man, and he bowed very low indeed before her.

Then he led them into his little room and locked the spectacles from the great box on all their eyes, just as he had done before. Afterward they passed on through the gate into the Emerald City, and when the people heard from the Guardian of the Gates that they had melted the Wicked Witch of the West they all gathered around the travellers and followed them in a great crowd to the Palace of Oz.

The soldier with the green whiskers was still on guard before the door, but he let them in at once and they were again met by the beautiful green girl, who showed each of them to their old rooms at once, so they might rest until the Great Oz was ready to receive them.

The soldier had the news carried straight to Oz that Dorothy and the other travellers had come back again, after destroying the Wicked Witch; but Oz made no reply. They thought the Great Wizard would send for them at once, but he did not. They had no word from him the next day, nor the next, nor the next. The waiting was tiresome and wearing, and at last they grew vexed that Oz should treat them in so poor a fashion, after sending them to undergo hardships and slavery. So the Scarecrow at last asked the green girl to take another message to Oz, saying if he did not let them in to see him at once they would call the Winged Monkeys to help them, and find out whether he kept his promises or not. When the Wizard was given this message he was so frightened that he sent word for them to come to the Throne Room at four minutes after nine o'clock the next morning. He had once met the Winged Monkeys in the Land of the West, and he did not wish to meet them again.

The four travellers passed a sleepless night, each thinking of the gift Oz had promised to bestow upon him. Dorothy fell asleep only once, and then she dreamed she was in Kansas, where Aunt Em was telling her how glad she was to have her little girl at home again.

Promptly at nine o'clock the next morning the green whiskered soldier came to them, and four minutes later they all went into the Throne Room of the Great Oz.

Of course each one of them expected to see the Wizard in the shape he had taken before, and all were greatly surprised when they looked about and saw no one at all in the room. They kept close to the door and closer to one another, for the stillness of the empty room was more dreadful than any of the forms they had seen Oz take.

Presently they heard a Voice, seeming to come from somewhere near the top of the great dome, and it said, solemnly,

"I am Oz, the Great and Terrible. Why do you seek me?"

They looked again in every part of the room, and then, seeing no one, Dorothy asked,

"Where are you?"

"I am everywhere," answered the Voice, "but to the eyes of common mortals I am invisible. I will now seat myself upon my throne, that you may converse with me." Indeed, the Voice seemed just then to come straight from the throne itself; so they walked toward it and stood in a row while Dorothy said:

"We have come to claim our promise, O Oz."

"What promise?" asked Oz.

"You promised to send me back to Kansas when the Wicked Witch was destroyed," said the girl.

"And you promised to give me brains," said the Scarecrow.

"And you promised to give me a heart," said the Tin Woodman.

"And you promised to give me courage," said the Cowardly Lion.

"Is the Wicked Witch really destroyed?" asked the Voice, and Dorothy thought it trembled a little.

"Yes," she answered, "I melted her with a bucket of water."

"Dear me," said the Voice; "how sudden! Well, come to me to-morrow, for I must have time to think it over."

"You've had plenty of time already," said the Tin Woodman, angrily.

"We shan't wait a day longer," said the Scarecrow.

"You must keep your promises to us!" exclaimed Dorothy.

The Lion thought it might be as well to frighten the Wizard, so he gave a large, loud roar, which was so fierce and dreadful that Toto jumped away from him in alarm and tipped over the screen that stood in a corner. As it fell with a crash they looked that way, and the next moment all of them were filled with wonder. For they saw, standing in just the spot the screen had hidden, a little, old man, with a bald head and a wrinkled face, who seemed to be as much surprised as they were. The Tin Woodman, raising his axe, rushed toward the little man and cried out,

"Who are you?"

"I am Oz, the Great and Terrible," said the little man, in a trembling voice, "but don't strike me—please don't!—and I'll do anything you want me to."

Our friends looked at him in surprise and dismay.

"I thought Oz was a great Head," said Dorothy.

"And I thought Oz was a lovely Lady," said the Scarecrow.

"And I thought Oz was a terrible Beast," said the Tin Woodman.

"And I thought Oz was a Ball of Fire," exclaimed the Lion.

"No; you are all wrong," said the little man, meekly. "I have been making believe."

"Making believe!" cried Dorothy. "Are you not a great Wizard?"

"Hush, my dear," he said; "don't speak so loud, or you will be overheard—and I should be ruined. I'm supposed to be a Great Wizard."

"And aren't you?" she asked.

"Not a bit of it, my dear; I'm just a common man."

"You're more than that," said the Scarecrow, in a grieved tone; "you're a humbug."

"Exactly so!" declared the little man, rubbing his hands together as if it pleased him; "I am a humbug."

"But this is terrible," said the Tin Woodman; "how shall I ever get my heart?"

"Or I my courage?" asked the Lion.

"Or I my brains?" wailed the Scarecrow, wiping the tears from his eyes with his coat-sleeve.

"My dear friends," said Oz, "I pray you not to speak of these little things. Think of me, and the terrible trouble I'm in at being found out."

"Doesn't anyone else know you're a humbug?" asked Dorothy.

"No one knows it but you four—and myself," replied Oz. "I have fooled everyone so long that I thought I should never be found out. It was a great mistake my ever letting you into the Throne Room. Usually I will not see even my subjects, and so they believe I am something terrible."

"But, I don't understand," said Dorothy, in bewilderment. "How was it that you appeared to me as a great Head?"

"That was one of my tricks," answered Oz. "Step this way, please, and I will tell you all about it."

He led the way to a small chamber in the rear of the Throne Room, and they all followed him. He pointed to one corner, in which lay the Great Head, made out of many thicknesses of paper, and with a carefully painted face.

"This I hung from the ceiling by a wire," said Oz; "I stood behind the screen and pulled a thread, to make the eyes move and the mouth open."

"But how about the voice?" she enquired.

"Oh, I am a ventriloquist," said the little man, "and I can throw the sound of my voice wherever I wish; so that you thought it was coming out of the Head. Here are the other things I used to deceive you." He showed the Scarecrow the dress and the mask he had worn when he seemed to be the lovely Lady; and the Tin Woodman saw that his Terrible Beast was nothing but a lot of skins, sewn together, with slats to keep their sides out. As for the Ball of Fire, the false Wizard had hung that also from the ceiling. It was really a ball of cotton, but when oil was poured upon it the ball burned fiercely.

"Really," said the Scarecrow, "you ought to be ashamed of yourself for being such a humbug."

"I am—I certainly am," answered the little man, sorrowfully; "but it was the only thing I could do. Sit down, please, there are plenty of chairs; and I will tell you my story."

So they sat down and listened while he told the following tale:

"I was born in Omaha—"

"Why, that isn't very far from Kansas!" cried Dorothy.

"No; but it's farther from here," he said, shaking his head at her, sadly. "When I grew up I became a ventriloquist, and at that I was very well trained by a great master. I can imitate any kind of a bird or beast." Here he mewed so like a kitten that Toto pricked up his ears and looked everywhere to see where she was. "After a time," continued Oz, "I tired of that, and became a balloonist."

"What is that?" asked Dorothy.

"A man who goes up in a balloon on circus day, so as to draw a crowd of people together and get them to pay to see the circus," he explained.

"Oh," she said; "I know."

"Well, one day I went up in a balloon and the ropes got twisted, so that I couldn't come down again. It went way up above the clouds, so far that a current of air struck it and carried it many, many miles away. For a day and a night I travelled through the air, and on the morning of the second day I awoke and found the balloon floating over a strange and beautiful country.

"It came down gradually, and I was not hurt a bit. But I found myself in the midst of a strange people, who, seeing me come from the clouds, thought I was a great Wizard. Of course I let them think so, because they were afraid of me, and promised to do anything I wished them to.

"Just to amuse myself, and keep the good people busy, I ordered them to build this City, and my palace; and they did it all willingly and well. Then I thought, as the country was so green and beautiful, I would call it the Emerald City, and to make the name fit better I put green spectacles on all the people, so that everything they saw was green."

"But isn't everything here green?" asked Dorothy.

"No more than in any other city," replied Oz; "but when you wear green spectacles, why of course everything you see looks green to you. The Emerald City was built a great many years ago, for I was a young man when the balloon brought me here, and I am a very old man now. But my people have worn green glasses on their eyes so long that most of them think it really is an Emerald City, and it certainly is a beautiful place, abounding in jewels and precious metals, and every good thing that is needed to make one happy. I have been good to the people, and they like me; but ever since this Palace was built I have shut myself up and would not see any of them.

"One of my greatest fears was the Witches, for while I had no magical powers at all I soon found out that the Witches were really able to do wonderful things. There were four of them in this country, and they ruled the people who live in the North and South and East and West. Fortunately, the Witches of the North and South were good, and I knew they would do me no harm; but the Witches of the East and West were terribly wicked, and had they not thought I was more powerful than they themselves, they would surely have destroyed me. As it was, I lived in deadly fear of them for many years; so you can imagine how pleased I was when I heard your house had fallen on the Wicked Witch of the East. When you came to me I was willing to promise anything if you would only do away with the other Witch; but, now that you have melted her, I am ashamed to say that I cannot keep my promises."

"I think you are a very bad man," said Dorothy.

"Oh, no, my dear; I'm really a very good man; but I'm a very bad Wizard, I must admit."

"Can't you give me brains?" asked the Scarecrow.

"You don't need them. You are learning something every day. A baby has brains, but it doesn't know much. Experience is the only thing that brings knowledge, and the longer you are on earth the more experience you are sure to get."

"That may all be true," said the Scarecrow, "but I shall be very unhappy unless you give me brains."

The false wizard looked at him carefully.

"Well," he said, with a sigh, "I'm not much of a magician, as I said; but if you will come to me to-morrow morning, I will stuff your head with brains. I cannot tell you how to use them, however; you must find that out for yourself."

"Oh, thank you—thank you!" cried the Scarecrow. "I'll find a way to use them, never fear!"

"But how about my courage?" asked the Lion, anxiously.

"You have plenty of courage, I am sure," answered Oz. "All you need is confidence in yourself. There is no living thing that is not afraid when it faces danger. True courage is in facing danger when you are afraid, and that kind of courage you have in plenty."

"Perhaps I have, but I'm scared just the same," said the Lion. "I shall really be very unhappy unless you give me the sort of courage that makes one forget he is afraid."

"Very well; I will give you that sort of courage to-morrow," replied Oz.

"How about my heart?" asked the Tin Woodman.

"Why, as for that," answered Oz, "I think you are wrong to want a heart. It makes most people unhappy. If you only knew it, you are in luck not to have a heart."

"That must be a matter of opinion," said the Tin Woodman. "For my part, I will bear all the unhappiness without a murmur, if you will give me the heart."

"Very well," answered Oz, meekly. "Come to me to-morrow and you shall have a heart. I have played Wizard for so many years that I may as well continue the part a little longer."

"And now," said Dorothy, "how am I to get back to Kansas?"

"We shall have to think about that," replied the little man, "Give me two or three days to consider the matter and I'll try to find a way to carry you over the desert. In the meantime you shall all be treated as my guests, and while you live in the Palace my people will wait upon you and obey your slightest wish. There is only one thing I ask in return for my help—such as it is. You must keep my secret and tell no one I am a humbug."

They agreed to say nothing of what they had learned, and went back to their rooms in high spirits. Even Dorothy had hope that "The Great and Terrible Humbug," as she called him, would find a way to send her back to Kansas, and if he did that she was willing to forgive him everything.

"'I feel wise, indeed,' said the Scarecrow."

CHAPTER XVI

THE MAGIC ART OF THE GREAT HUMBUG

NEXT MORNING the Scarecrow said to his friends:
"Congratulate me. I am going to Oz to get my brains at last. When I return I shall be as other men are."

"I have always liked you as you were," said Dorothy, simply.

"It is kind of you to like a Scarecrow," he replied. "But surely you will think more of me when you hear the splendid thoughts my new brain is going to turn out." Then he said good-bye to them all in a cheerful voice and went to the Throne Room, where he rapped upon the door.

"Come in," said Oz.

The Scarecrow went in and found the little man sitting down by the window, engaged in deep thought.

"I have come for my brains," remarked the Scarecrow, a little uneasily.

"Oh, yes; sit down in that chair, please," replied Oz. "You must excuse me for taking your head off, but I shall have to do it in order to put your brains in their proper place."

"That's all right," said the Scarecrow. "You are quite welcome to take my head off, as long as it will be a better one when you put it on again."

So the Wizard unfastened his head and emptied out the straw. Then he entered the back room and took up a measure of bran, which he mixed with a great many pins and needles. Having shaken them together thoroughly, he filled the top of the Scarecrow's head with the mixture and stuffed the rest of the space with straw, to hold it in place. When he had fastened the Scarecrow's head on his body again he said to him,

"Hereafter you will be a great man, for I have given you a lot of bran-new brains."

The Scarecrow was both pleased and proud at the fulfillment of his greatest wish, and having thanked Oz warmly he went back to his friends.

Dorothy looked at him curiously. His head was quite bulging out at the top with brains.

"How do you feel?" she asked.

"I feel wise, indeed," he answered, earnestly. "When I get used to my brains I shall know everything."

"Why are those needles and pins sticking out of your head?" asked the Tin Woodman.

"That is proof that he is sharp," remarked the Lion.

"Well, I must go to Oz and get my heart," said the Woodman. So he walked to the Throne Room and knocked at the door.

"Come in," called Oz, and the Woodman entered and said,

"I have come for my heart."

"Very well," answered the little man. "But I shall have to cut a hole in your breast, so I can put your heart in the right place. I hope it won't hurt you."

"Oh, no;" answered the Woodman. "I shall not feel it at all."

So Oz brought a pair of tinners' shears and cut a small, square hole in the left side of the Tin Woodman's breast. Then, going to a chest of drawers, he took out a pretty heart, made entirely of silk and stuffed with sawdust.

"Isn't it a beauty?" he asked.

"It is, indeed!" replied the Woodman, who was greatly pleased. "But is it a kind heart?"

"Oh, very!" answered Oz. He put the heart in the Woodman's breast and then replaced the square of tin, soldering it neatly together where it had been cut.

"There," said he; "now you have a heart that any man might be proud of. I'm sorry I had to put a patch on your breast, but it really couldn't be helped."

"Never mind the patch," exclaimed the happy Woodman. "I am very grateful to you, and shall never forget your kindness."

"Don't speak of it," replied Oz.

Then the Tin Woodman went back to his friends, who wished him every joy on account of his good fortune.

The Lion now walked to the Throne Room and knocked at the door.

"Come in," said Oz.

"I have come for my courage," announced the Lion, entering the room.

"Very well," answered the little man; "I will get it for you."

He went to a cupboard and reaching up to a high shelf took down a square green bottle, the contents of which he poured into a green-gold dish, beautifully carved. Placing this before the Cowardly Lion, who sniffed at it as if he did not like it, the Wizard said,

"Drink."

"What is it?" asked the Lion.

"Well," answered Oz, "if it were inside of you, it would be courage. You know, of course, that courage is always inside one; so that this really cannot be called courage until you have swallowed it. Therefore I advise you to drink it as soon as possible."

The Lion hesitated no longer, but drank till the dish was empty.

"How do you feel now?" asked Oz.

"Full of courage," replied the Lion, who went joyfully back to his friends to tell them of his good fortune.

Oz, left to himself, smiled to think of his success in giving the Scarecrow and the Tin Woodman and the Lion exactly what they thought they wanted. "How can I help being a humbug," he said, "when all these people make me do things that everybody knows can't be done? It was easy to make the Scarecrow and the Lion and the Woodman happy, because they imagined I could do anything. But it will take more than imagination to carry Dorothy back to Kansas, and I'm sure I don't know how it can be done."

CHAPTER XVII

HOW THE BALLOON WAS LAUNCHED

FOR THREE days Dorothy heard nothing from Oz. These were sad days for the little girl, although her friends were all quite happy and contented. The Scarecrow told them there were wonderful thoughts in his head; but he would not say what they were because he knew no one could understand them but himself. When the Tin Woodman walked about he felt his heart rattling around in his breast; and he told Dorothy he had discovered it to be a kinder and more tender heart than the one he had owned when he was made of flesh. The Lion declared he was afraid of nothing on earth, and would gladly face an army of men or a dozen of the fierce Kalidahs.

Thus each of the little party was satisfied except Dorothy, who longed more than ever to get back to Kansas.

On the fourth day, to her great joy, Oz sent for her, and when she entered the Throne Room he said, pleasantly:

"Sit down, my dear; I think I have found the way to get you out of this country."

"And back to Kansas?" she asked, eagerly.

"Well, I'm not sure about Kansas," said Oz; "for I haven't the faintest notion which way it lies. But the first thing to do is to cross the desert, and then it should be easy to find your way home."

"How can I cross the desert?" she enquired.

"Well, I'll tell you what I think," said the little man. "You see, when I came to this country it was in a balloon. You also came through the air, being carried by a cyclone. So I believe the best way to get across the desert will be through the air. Now, it is quite beyond my powers to make a cyclone; but I've been thinking the matter over, and I believe I can make a balloon."

"How?" asked Dorothy.

"A balloon," said Oz, "is made of silk, which is coated with glue to keep the gas in it. I have plenty of silk in the Palace, so it will be no trouble for us to make the balloon. But in all this country there is no gas to fill the balloon with, to make it float."

"If it won't float," remarked Dorothy, "it will be of no use to us."

"True," answered Oz. "But there is another way to make it float, which is to fill it with hot air. Hot air isn't as good as gas, for if the air should get cold the balloon would come down in the desert, and we should be lost."

"We!" exclaimed the girl; "are you going with me?"

"Yes, of course," replied Oz. "I am tired of being such a humbug. If I should go out of this Palace my people would soon discover I am not a Wizard, and then they would be vexed with me for having deceived them. So I have to stay shut up in these rooms all day, and it gets tiresome. I'd much rather go back to Kansas with you and be in a circus again."

"I shall be glad to have your company," said Dorothy.

"Thank you," he answered. "Now, if you will help me sew the silk together, we will begin to work on our balloon."

So Dorothy took a needle and thread, and as fast as Oz cut the strips of silk into proper shape the girl sewed them neatly together. First there was a strip of light green silk, then a strip of dark green and then a strip of emerald green; for Oz had a fancy to make the balloon in different shades of the color about them. It took three days to sew all the strips together, but when it was finished they had a big bag of green silk more than twenty feet long.

Then Oz painted it on the inside with a coat of thin glue, to make it air-tight, after which he announced that the balloon was ready.

"But we must have a basket to ride in," he said. So he sent the soldier with the green whiskers for a big clothes basket, which he fastened with many ropes to the bottom of the balloon.

When it was all ready, Oz sent word to his people that he was going to make a visit to a great brother Wizard who lived in the clouds. The news spread rapidly throughout the city and everyone came to see the wonderful sight.

Oz ordered the balloon carried out in front of the Palace,

and the people gazed upon it with much curiosity. The Tin Woodman had chopped a big pile of wood, and now he made a fire of it, and Oz held the bottom of the balloon over the fire so that the hot air that arose from it would be caught in the silken bag. Gradually the balloon swelled out and rose into the air, until finally the basket just touched the ground.

Then Oz got into the basket and said to all the people in a loud voice:

"I am now going away to make a visit. While I am gone the Scarecrow will rule over you. I command you to obey him as you would me."

The balloon was by this time tugging hard at the rope that held it to the ground, for the air within it was hot, and this made it so much lighter in weight than the air without that it pulled hard to rise into the sky.

"Come, Dorothy!" cried the Wizard; "hurry up, or the balloon will fly away."

"I can't find Toto anywhere," replied Dorothy, who did not wish to leave her little dog behind. Toto had run into the crowd to bark at a kitten, and Dorothy at last found him. She picked him up and ran toward the balloon.

She was within a few steps of it, and Oz was holding out his hands to help her into the basket, when, crack! went the ropes, and the balloon rose into the air without her.

"Come back!" she screamed; "I want to go, too!"

"I can't come back, my dear," called Oz from the basket. "Good-bye!"

"Good-bye!" shouted everyone, and all eyes were turned

upward to where the Wizard was riding in the basket, rising every moment farther and farther into the sky.

And that was the last any of them ever saw of Oz, the Wonderful Wizard, though he may have reached Omaha safely, and be there now, for all we know. But the people remembered him lovingly, and said to one another,

"Oz was always our friend. When he was here he built for us this beautiful Emerald City, and now he is gone he has left the Wise Scarecrow to rule over us."

Still, for many days they grieved over the loss of the Wonderful Wizard, and would not be comforted.

"The Scarecrow sat on the big throne."

CHAPTER XVIII

AWAY TO THE SOUTH

DOROTHY WEPT bitterly at the passing of her hope to get home to Kansas again; but when she thought it all over she was glad she had not gone up in a balloon. And she also felt sorry at losing Oz, and so did her companions.

The Tin Woodman came to her and said,

"Truly I should be ungrateful if I failed to mourn for the man who gave me my lovely heart. I should like to cry a little because Oz is gone, if you will kindly wipe away my tears, so that I shall not rust."

"With pleasure," she answered, and brought a towel at once. Then the Tin Woodman wept for several minutes, and she watched the tears carefully and wiped them away with the towel. When he had finished he thanked her kindly and oiled himself thoroughly with his jewelled oil-can, to guard against mishap.

The Scarecrow was now the ruler of the Emerald City, and although he was not a Wizard the people were proud of him. "For," they said, "there is not another city in all the world that is ruled by a stuffed man." And, so far as they knew, they were quite right.

The morning after the balloon had gone up with Oz the four travellers met in the Throne Room and talked matters over. The Scarecrow sat in the big throne and the others stood respectfully before him.

"We are not so unlucky," said the new ruler; "for this Palace and the Emerald City belong to us, and we can do just as we please. When I remember that a short time ago I was up on a pole in a farmer's cornfield, and that I am now the ruler of this beautiful City, I am quite satisfied with my lot."

"I also," said the Tin Woodman, "am well pleased with my new heart; and, really, that was the only thing I wished in all the world."

"For my part, I am content in knowing I am as brave as any beast that ever lived, if not braver," said the Lion, modestly.

"If Dorothy would only be contented to live in the Emerald City," continued the Scarecrow, "we might all be happy together."

"But I don't want to live here," cried Dorothy. "I want to go to Kansas, and live with Aunt Em and Uncle Henry."

"Well, then, what can be done?" enquired the Woodman.

The Scarecrow decided to think, and he thought so hard

that the pins and needles began to stick out of his brains. Finally he said:

"Why not call the Winged Monkeys, and ask them to carry you over the desert?"

"I never thought of that!" said Dorothy, joyfully. "It's just the thing. I'll go at once for the Golden Cap."

When she brought it into the Throne Room she spoke the magic words, and soon the band of Winged Monkeys flew in through an open window and stood beside her.

"This is the second time you have called us," said the Monkey King, bowing before the little girl. "What do you wish?"

"I want you to fly with me to Kansas," said Dorothy.

But the Monkey King shook his head.

"That cannot be done," he said. "We belong to this country alone, and cannot leave it. There has never been a Winged Monkey in Kansas yet, and I suppose there never will be, for they don't belong there. We shall be glad to serve you in any way in our power, but we cannot cross the desert. Good-bye."

And with another bow the Monkey King spread his wings and flew away through the window, followed by all his band.

Dorothy was almost ready to cry with disappointment.

"I have wasted the charm of the Golden Cap to no purpose," she said, "for the Winged Monkeys cannot help me."

"It is certainly too bad!" said the tender hearted Woodman.

The Scarecrow was thinking again, and his head bulged out so horribly that Dorothy feared it would burst.

"Let us call in the soldier with the green whiskers," he said, "and ask his advice."

So the soldier was summoned and entered the Throne Room timidly, for while Oz was alive he never was allowed to come further than the door.

"This little girl," said the Scarecrow to the soldier, "wishes to cross the desert. How can she do so?"

"I cannot tell," answered the soldier; "for nobody has ever crossed the desert, unless it is Oz himself."

"Is there no one who can help me?" asked Dorothy, earnestly.

"Glinda might," he suggested.

"Who is Glinda?" enquired the Scarecrow.

"The Witch of the South. She is the most powerful of all the Witches, and rules over the Quadlings. Besides, her castle stands on the edge of the desert, so she may know a way to cross it."

"Glinda is a good Witch, isn't she?" asked the child.

"The Quadlings think she is good," said the soldier, "and she is kind to everyone. I have heard that Glinda is a beautiful woman, who knows how to keep young in spite of the many years she has lived."

"How can I get to her castle?" asked Dorothy.

"The road is straight to the South," he answered, "but it is said to be full of dangers to travellers. There are wild beasts in the woods, and a race of queer men who do not like strangers to cross their country. For this reason none of the Quadlings ever come to the Emerald City."

The soldier then left them and the Scarecrow said, "It seems, in spite of dangers, that the best thing

Dorothy can do is to travel to the Land of the South and ask Glinda to help her. For, of course, if Dorothy stays here she will never get back to Kansas."

"You must have been thinking again," remarked the Tin Woodman.

"I have," said the Scarecrow.

"I shall go with Dorothy," declared the Lion, "for I am tired of your city and long for the woods and the country again. I am really a wild beast, you know. Besides, Dorothy will need someone to protect her."

"That is true," agreed the Woodman. "My axe may be of service to her; so I, also, will go with her to the Land of the South."

"When shall we start?" asked the Scarecrow.

"Are you going?" they asked, in surprise.

"Certainly. If it wasn't for Dorothy I should never have had brains. She lifted me from the pole in the cornfield and brought me to the Emerald City. So my good luck is all due to her, and I shall never leave her until she starts back to Kansas for good and all."

"Thank you," said Dorothy, gratefully. "You are all very kind to me. But I should like to start as soon as possible."

"We shall go to-morrow morning," returned the Scarecrow. "So now let us all get ready, for it will be a long journey."

"*The branches bent down and twined around him.*"

CHAPTER XIX

ATTACKED BY THE FIGHTING TREES

T HE NEXT morning Dorothy kissed the pretty green girl good-bye, and they all shook hands with the soldier with the green whiskers, who had walked with them as far as the gate. When the Guardian of the Gate saw them again he wondered greatly that they could leave the beautiful City to get into new trouble. But he at once unlocked their spectacles, which he put back into the green box, and gave them many good wishes to carry with them.

"You are now our ruler," he said to the Scarecrow; "so you must come back to us as soon as possible."

"I certainly shall if I am able," the Scarecrow replied; "but I must help Dorothy to get home, first."

As Dorothy bade the good-natured Guardian a last farewell she said,

"I have been very kindly treated in your lovely City, and everyone has been good to me. I cannot tell you how grateful I am."

"Don't try, my dear," he answered. "We should like to keep you with us, but if it is your wish to return to Kansas I hope you will find a way." He then opened the gate of the outer wall and they walked forth and started upon their journey.

The sun shone brightly as our friends turned their faces toward the Land of the South. They were all in the best of spirits, and laughed and chatted together. Dorothy was once more filled with the hope of getting home, and the Scarecrow and the Tin Woodman were glad to be of use to her. As for the Lion, he sniffed the fresh air with delight and whisked his tail from side to side in pure joy at being in the country again, while Toto ran around them and chased the moths and butterflies, barking merrily all the time.

"City life does not agree with me at all," remarked the Lion, as they walked along at a brisk pace. "I have lost much flesh since I lived there, and now I am anxious for a chance to show the other beasts how courageous I have grown."

They now turned and took a last look at the Emerald City. All they could see was a mass of towers and steeples behind the green walls, and high up above everything the spires and dome of the Palace of Oz.

"Oz was not such a bad Wizard, after all," said the Tin Woodman, as he felt his heart rattling around in his breast.

"He knew how to give me brains, and very good brains, too," said the Scarecrow.

"If Oz had taken a dose of the same courage he gave me," added the Lion, "he would have been a brave man."

Dorothy said nothing. Oz had not kept the promise he made her, but he had done his best, so she forgave him. As he said, he was a good man, even if he was a bad Wizard.

The first day's journey was through the green fields and bright flowers that stretched about the Emerald City on every side. They slept that night on the grass, with nothing but the stars over them; and they rested very well indeed.

In the morning they travelled on until they came to a thick wood. There was no way of going around it, for it seemed to extend to the right and left as far as they could see; and, besides, they did not dare change the direction of their journey for fear of getting lost. So they looked for the place where it would be easiest to get into the forest.

The Scarecrow, who was in the lead, finally discovered a big tree with such wide spreading branches that there was room for the party to pass underneath. So he walked forward to the tree, but just as he came under the first branches they bent down and twined around him, and the next minute he was raised from the ground and flung headlong among his fellow travellers.

This did not hurt the Scarecrow, but it surprised him, and he looked rather dizzy when Dorothy picked him up.

"Here is another space between the trees," called the Lion.

"Let me try it first," said the Scarecrow, "for it doesn't hurt me to get thrown about." He walked up to another tree, as he spoke, but its branches immediately seized him and tossed him back again.

"This is strange," exclaimed Dorothy; "what shall we do?"

"The trees seem to have made up their minds to fight us, and stop our journey," remarked the Lion.

"I believe I will try it myself," said the Woodman, and shouldering his axe he marched up to the first tree that had handled the Scarecrow so roughly. When a big branch bent down to seize him the Woodman chopped at it so fiercely that he cut it in two. At once the tree began shaking all its branches as if in pain, and the Tin Woodman passed safely under it.

"Come on!" he shouted to the others; "be quick!"

They all ran forward and passed under the tree without injury, except Toto, who was caught by a small branch and shaken until he howled. But the Woodman promptly chopped off the branch and set the little dog free.

The other trees of the forest did nothing to keep them back, so they made up their minds that only the first row of trees could bend down their branches, and that probably these were the policemen of the forest, and given this wonderful power in order to keep strangers out of it.

The four travellers walked with ease through the trees until they came to the further edge of the wood. Then, to their surprise, they found before them a high wall, which seemed to be made of white china. It was smooth, like the surface of a dish, and higher than their heads.

"What shall we do now?" asked Dorothy.

"I will make a ladder," said the Tin Woodman, "for we certainly must climb over the wall."

" These people were all made of china."

CHAPTER XX

THE DAINTY
CHINA COUNTRY

W HILE THE woodman was making a ladder from wood which he found in the forest Dorothy lay down and slept, for she was tired by the long walk. The Lion also curled himself up to sleep and Toto lay beside him.

The Scarecrow watched the Woodman while he worked, and said to him:

"I cannot think why this wall is here, nor what it is made of."

"Rest your brains and do not worry about the wall," replied the Woodman; "when we have climbed over it we shall know what is on the other side."

After a time the ladder was finished. It looked clumsy, but the Tin Woodman was sure it was strong and would answer their purpose. The Scarecrow waked Dorothy and the Lion and Toto, and told them that the ladder was ready. The Scarecrow climbed up the ladder first, but he was so awkward that Dorothy had to follow close behind and keep him from falling off. When he got his head over the top of the wall the Scarecrow said,

"Oh, my!"

"Go on," exclaimed Dorothy.

So the Scarecrow climbed further up and sat down on the top of the wall, and Dorothy put her head over and cried,

"Oh, my!" just as the Scarecrow had done.

Then Toto came up, and immediately began to bark, but Dorothy made him be still.

The Lion climbed the ladder next, and the Tin Woodman came last; but both of them cried, "Oh, my!" as soon as they looked over the wall. When they were all sitting in a row on the top of the wall they looked down and saw a strange sight.

Before them was a great stretch of country having a floor as smooth and shining and white as the bottom of a big platter. Scattered around were many houses made entirely of china and painted in the brightest colours. These houses were quite small, the biggest of them reaching only as high as Dorothy's waist. There were also pretty little barns, with china fences around them, and many cows and sheep and horses and pigs and chickens, all made of china, were standing about in groups.

But the strangest of all were the people who lived in this queer country. There were milk-maids and shepherdesses, with bright-colored bodices and golden spots all over their gowns; and princesses with most gorgeous frocks of silver and gold and purple; and shepherds dressed in knee-breeches with pink and yellow and blue stripes down them, and golden buckles on their shoes; and princes with jew-elled crowns upon their heads, wearing ermine robes and satin doublets; and funny clowns in ruffled gowns, with round red spots upon their cheeks and tall, pointed caps. And, strangest of all, these people were all made of china, even to their clothes, and were so small that the tallest of them was no higher than Dorothy's knee.

No one did so much as look at the travellers at first, except one little purple china dog with an extra-large head, which came to the wall and barked at them in a tiny voice, afterwards running away again.

"How shall we get down?" asked Dorothy.

They found the ladder so heavy they could not pull it up, so the Scarecrow fell off the wall and the others jumped down upon him so that the hard floor would not hurt their feet. Of course they took pains not to light on his head and get the pins in their feet. When all were safely down they picked up the Scarecrow, whose body was quite flattened out, and patted his straw into shape again.

"We must cross this strange place in order to get to the other side," said Dorothy; "for it would be unwise for us to go any other way except due South."

They began walking through the country of the china people, and the first thing they came to was a china milk-maid milking a china cow. As they drew near the cow sud-denly gave a kick and kicked over the stool, the pail, and even the milk-maid herself, all falling on the china ground with a great clatter.

Dorothy was shocked to see that the cow had broken her leg short off, and that the pail was lying in several small pieces, while the poor milk-maid had a nick in her left elbow.

"There!" cried the milk-maid, angrily; "see what you have done! My cow has broken her leg, and I must take her to the mender's shop and have it glued on again. What do you mean by coming here and frightening my cow?"

"I'm very sorry," returned Dorothy; "please forgive us."

But the pretty milk-maid was much too vexed to make any answer. She picked up the leg sulkily and led her cow away, the poor animal limping on three legs. As she left them the milk-maid cast many reproachful glances over her shoulder at the clumsy strangers, holding her nicked elbow close to her side.

Dorothy was quite grieved at this mishap.

"We must be very careful here," said the kind-hearted Woodman, "or we may hurt these pretty little people so they will never get over it."

A little farther on Dorothy met a most beautifully dressed young princess, who stopped short as she saw the strangers and started to run away.

Dorothy wanted to see more of the Princess, so she ran after her; but the china girl cried out,

"Don't chase me! don't chase me!"

She had such a frightened little voice that Dorothy stopped and said,

"Why not?"

"Because," answered the princess, also stopping, a safe distance away, "if I run I may fall down and break myself."

"But couldn't you be mended?" asked the girl.

"Oh, yes; but one is never so pretty after being mended, you know," replied the princess.

"I suppose not," said Dorothy.

"Now there is Mr. Joker, one of our clowns," continued the china lady, "who is always trying to stand upon his head. He has broken himself so often that he is mended in a hundred places, and doesn't look at all pretty. Here he comes now, so you can see for yourself."

Indeed, a jolly little Clown now came walking toward them, and Dorothy could see that in spite of his pretty clothes of red and yellow and green he was completely covered with cracks, running every which way and showing plainly that he had been mended in many places.

The Clown put his hands in his pockets, and after puffing out his cheeks and nodding his head at them saucily he said,

> "My lady fair,
> Why do you stare
> At poor old Mr. Joker?
> You're quite as stiff
> And prim as if
> You'd eaten up a poker!"

"Be quiet, sir!" said the princess; "can't you see these are strangers, and should be treated with respect?"

"Well, that's respect, I expect," declared the Clown, and immediately stood upon his head.

"Don't mind Mr. Joker," said the princess to Dorothy: "he is considerably cracked in his head, and that makes him foolish."

"Oh, I don't mind him a bit," said Dorothy. "But you are so beautiful," she continued, "that I am sure I could love you dearly. Won't you let me carry you back to Kansas and stand you on Aunt Em's mantle-shelf? I could carry you in my basket."

"That would make me very unhappy," answered the china princess. "You see, here in our own country we live contentedly, and can talk and move around as we please. But whenever any of us are taken away our joints at once stiffen, and we can only stand straight and look pretty. Of course that is all that is expected of us when we are on mantle-shelves and cabinets and drawing-room tables, but our lives are much pleasanter here in our own country."

"I would not make you unhappy for all the world!" exclaimed Dorothy; "so I'll just say good-bye."

"Good-bye," replied the princess.

They walked carefully through the china country. The little animals and all the people scampered out of their way, fearing the strangers would break them, and after an hour or so the travellers reached the other side of the country and came to another china wall.

It was not as high as the first, however, and by standing upon the Lion's back they all managed to scramble to the top. Then the Lion gathered his legs under him and jumped on the wall; but just as he jumped he upset a china church with his tail and smashed it all to pieces.

"That was too bad," said Dorothy, "but really I think we

were lucky in not doing these little people more harm than breaking a cow's leg and a church. They are all so brittle!"

"They are, indeed," said the Scarecrow, "and I am thankful I am made of straw and cannot be easily damaged. There are worse things in the world than being a Scarecrow."

CHAPTER XXI

THE LION BECOMES
THE KING OF BEASTS

AFTER CLIMBING down from the china wall the travellers found themselves in a disagreeable country, full of bogs and marshes and covered with tall, rank grass. It was difficult to walk far without falling into muddy holes, for the grass was so thick that it hid them from sight. However, by carefully picking their way, they got safely along until they reached solid ground. But here the country seemed wilder than ever, and after a long and tiresome walk through the underbrush they entered another forest, where the trees were bigger and older than any they had ever seen.

"This forest is perfectly delightful," declared the Lion, looking around him with joy; "never have I seen a more beautiful place."

"It seems gloomy," said the Scarecrow.

"Not a bit of it," answered the Lion; "I should like to live here all my life. See how soft the dried leaves are under your feet and how rich and green the moss is that clings to these old trees. Surely no wild beast could wish a pleasanter home."

"Perhaps there are wild beasts in the forest now," said Dorothy.

"I suppose there are," returned the Lion; "but I do not see any of them about."

They walked through the forest until it became too dark to go any farther. Dorothy and Toto and the Lion lay down to sleep, while the Woodman and the Scarecrow kept watch over them as usual.

When morning came they started again. Before they had gone far they heard a low rumble, as of the growling of many wild animals. Toto whimpered a little but none of the others was frightened and they kept along the well-trodden path until they came to an opening in the wood, in which were gathered hundreds of beasts of every variety. There were tigers and elephants and bears and wolves and foxes and all the others in the natural history, and for a moment Dorothy was afraid. But the Lion explained that the animals were holding a meeting, and he judged by their snarling and growling that they were in great trouble.

As he spoke several of the beasts caught sight of him, and at once the great assemblage hushed as if by magic. The biggest of the tigers came up to the Lion and bowed, saying,

"Welcome, O King of Beasts! You have come in good time to fight our enemy and bring peace to all the animals of the forest once more."

"What is your trouble?" asked the Lion, quietly.

"We are all threatened," answered the tiger, "by a fierce enemy which has lately come into this forest. It is a most tremendous monster, like a great spider, with a body as big as an elephant and legs as long as a tree trunk. It has eight of these long legs, and as the monster crawls through the forest he seizes an animal with a leg and drags it to his mouth, where he eats it as a spider does a fly. Not one of us is safe while this fierce creature is alive, and we had called a meeting to decide how to take care of ourselves when you came among us."

The Lion thought for a moment.

"Are there any other lions in this forest?" he asked.

"No; there were some, but the monster has eaten them all. And, besides, they were none of them nearly so large and brave as you."

"If I put an end to your enemy will you bow down to me and obey me as King of the Forest?" enquired the Lion.

"We will do that gladly," returned the tiger; and all the other beasts roared with a mighty roar: "We will!"

"Where is this great spider of yours now?" asked the Lion.

"Yonder, among the oak trees," said the tiger, pointing with his fore-foot.

"Take good care of these friends of mine," said the Lion, "and I will go at once to fight the monster."

He bade his comrades good-bye and marched proudly away to do battle with the enemy.

The great spider was lying asleep when the Lion found him, and it looked so ugly that its foe turned up his nose in disgust. Its legs were quite as long as the tiger had said, and its body covered with coarse black hair. It had a great mouth, with a row of sharp teeth a foot long; but its head was joined to the pudgy body by a neck as slender as a wasp's waist. This gave the Lion a hint of the best way to attack the creature, and as he knew it was easier to fight it asleep than awake, he gave a great spring and landed directly upon the monster's back. Then, with one blow of his heavy paw, all armed with sharp claws, he knocked the spider's head from its body. Jumping down, he watched it until the long legs stopped wiggling, when he knew it was quite dead.

The Lion went back to the opening where the beasts of the forest were waiting for him and said, proudly,

"You need fear your enemy no longer."

Then the beasts bowed down to the Lion as their King, and he promised to come back and rule over them as soon as Dorothy was safely on her way to Kansas.

" The Head shot forward and struck the Scarecrow."

CHAPTER XXII

THE COUNTRY OF THE QUADLINGS

T HE FOUR travellers passed through the rest of the forest in safety, and when they came out from its gloom saw before them a steep hill, covered from top to bottom with great pieces of rock.

"That will be a hard climb," said the Scarecrow, "but we must get over the hill, nevertheless."

So he led the way and the others followed. They had nearly reached the first rock when they heard a rough voice cry out,

"Keep back!"

"Who are you?" asked the Scarecrow. Then a head showed itself over the rock and the same voice said,

"This hill belongs to us, and we don't allow anyone to cross it."

"But we must cross it," said the Scarecrow. "We're going to the country of the Quadlings."

"But you shall not!" replied the voice, and there stepped from behind the rock the strangest man the travellers had ever seen.

He was quite short and stout and had a big head, which was flat at the top and supported by a thick neck full of wrinkles. But he had no arms at all, and, seeing this, the Scarecrow did not fear that so helpless a creature could prevent them from climbing the hill. So he said,

"I'm sorry not to do as you wish, but we must pass over your hill whether you like it or not," and he walked boldly forward.

As quick as lightning the man's head shot forward and his neck stretched out until the top of the head, where it was flat, struck the Scarecrow in the middle and sent him tumbling, over and over, down the hill. Almost as quickly as it came the head went back to the body, and the man laughed harshly as he said,

"It isn't as easy as you think!"

A chorus of boisterous laughter came from the other rocks, and Dorothy saw hundreds of the armless Hammer-Heads upon the hillside, one behind every rock.

The Lion became quite angry at the laughter caused by the Scarecrow's mishap, and giving a loud roar that echoed like thunder he dashed up the hill.

Again a head shot swiftly out, and the great Lion went rolling down the hill as if he had been struck by a cannon ball.

Dorothy ran down and helped the Scarecrow to his feet, and the Lion came up to her, feeling rather bruised and sore, and said,

"It is useless to fight people with shooting heads; no one can withstand them."

"What can we do, then?" she asked.

"Call the Winged Monkeys," suggested the Tin Woodman; "you have still the right to command them once more."

"Very well," she answered, and putting on the Golden Cap she uttered the magic words. The Monkeys were as prompt as ever, and in a few moments the entire band stood before her.

"What are your commands?" enquired the King of the Monkeys, bowing low.

"Carry us over the hill to the country of the Quadlings," answered the girl.

"It shall be done," said the King, and at once the Winged Monkeys caught the four travellers and Toto up in their arms and flew away with them. As they passed over the hill the Hammer-Heads yelled with vexation, and shot their heads high in the air; but they could not reach the Winged Monkeys, which carried Dorothy and her comrades safely over the hill and set them down in the beautiful country of the Quadlings.

"This is the last time you can summon us," said the leader to Dorothy; "so good-bye and good luck to you."

"Good-bye, and thank you very much," returned the girl; and the Monkeys rose into the air and were out of sight in a twinkling.

The country of the Quadlings seemed rich and happy. There was field upon field of ripening grain, with well-paved roads running between, and pretty rippling brooks with strong bridges across them. The fences and houses and bridges were all painted bright red, just as they had been painted yellow in the country of the Winkies and blue in the country of the Munchkins. The Quadlings themselves, who were short and fat and looked chubby and good natured, were dressed all in red, which showed bright against the green grass and the yellowing grain.

The Monkeys had set them down near a farm house, and the four travellers walked up to it and knocked at the door. It was opened by the farmer's wife, and when Dorothy asked for something to eat the woman gave them all a good dinner, with three kinds of cake and four kinds of cookies, and a bowl of milk for Toto.

"How far is it to the Castle of Glinda?" asked the child.

"It is not a great way," answered the farmer's wife. "Take the road to the South and you will soon reach it."

Thanking the good woman, they started afresh and walked by the fields and across the pretty bridges until they saw before them a very beautiful Castle. Before the gates were three young girls, dressed in handsome red uniforms trimmed with gold braid; and as Dorothy approached one of them said to her,

"Why have you come to the South Country?"

"To see the Good Witch who rules here," she answered. "Will you take me to her?"

"Let me have your name and I will ask Glinda if she will

receive you." They told who they were, and the girl soldier went into the Castle. After a few moments she came back to say that Dorothy and the others were to be admitted at once.

" You must give me the Golden Cap."

CHAPTER XXIII

THE GOOD WITCH GRANTS DOROTHY'S WISH

BEFORE THEY went to see Glinda, however, they were taken to a room of the Castle, where Dorothy washed her face and combed her hair, and the Lion shook the dust out of his mane, and the Scarecrow patted himself into his best shape, and the Woodman polished his tin and oiled his joints.

When they were all quite presentable they followed the soldier girl into a big room where the Witch Glinda sat upon a throne of rubies.

She was both beautiful and young to their eyes. Her hair was a rich red in color and fell in flowing ringlets over her shoulders. Her dress was pure white; but her eyes were blue, and they looked kindly upon the little girl.

"What can I do for you, my child?" she asked.

Dorothy told the Witch all her story; how the cyclone had brought her to the Land of Oz, how she had found her companions, and of the wonderful adventures they had met with.

"My greatest wish now," she added, "is to get back to Kansas, for Aunt Em will surely think something dreadful has happened to me, and that will make her put on mourning; and unless the crops are better this year than they were last I am sure Uncle Henry cannot afford it."

Glinda leaned forward and kissed the sweet, upturned face of the loving little girl.

"Bless your dear heart," she said, "I am sure I can tell you of a way to get back to Kansas." Then she added:

"But, if I do, you must give me the Golden Cap."

"Willingly!" exclaimed Dorothy; "indeed, it is of no use to me now, and when you have it you can command the Winged Monkeys three times."

"And I think I shall need their service just those three times," answered Glinda, smiling.

Dorothy then gave her the Golden Cap, and the Witch said to the Scarecrow,

"What will you do when Dorothy has left us?"

"I will return to the Emerald City," he replied, "for Oz has made me its ruler and the people like me. The only thing that worries me is how to cross the hill of the Hammer-Heads."

"By means of the Golden Cap I shall command the Winged Monkeys to carry you to the gates of the Emerald City," said Glinda, "for it would be a shame to deprive the people of so wonderful a ruler."

"Am I really wonderful?" asked the Scarecrow.

"You are unusual," replied Glinda.

Turning to the Tin Woodman, she asked:

"What will become of you when Dorothy leaves this country?"

He leaned on his axe and thought a moment. Then he said,

"The Winkies were very kind to me, and wanted me to rule over them after the Wicked Witch died. I am fond of the Winkies, and if I could get back again to the country of the West I should like nothing better than to rule over them forever."

"My second command to the Winged Monkeys," said Glinda, "will be that they carry you safely to the land of the Winkies. Your brains may not be so large to look at as those of the Scarecrow, but you are really brighter than he is—when you are well polished—and I am sure you will rule the Winkies wisely and well."

Then the Witch looked at the big, shaggy Lion and asked,

"When Dorothy has returned to her own home, what will become of you?"

"Over the hill of the Hammer-Heads," he answered, "lies a grand old forest, and all the beasts that live there have made me their King. If I could only get back to this forest I would pass my life very happily there."

"My third command to the Winged Monkeys," said Glinda, "shall be to carry you to your forest. Then, having used up the powers of the Golden Cap, I shall give it to the King of the Monkeys, that he and his band may thereafter be free for evermore."

The Scarecrow and the Tin Woodman and the Lion now thanked the Good Witch earnestly for her kindness, and Dorothy exclaimed,

"You are certainly as good as you are beautiful! But you have not yet told me how to get back to Kansas."

"Your Silver Shoes will carry you over the desert," replied Glinda. "If you had known their power you could have gone back to your Aunt Em the very first day you came to this country."

"But then I should not have had my wonderful brains!" cried the Scarecrow. "I might have passed my whole life in the farmer's cornfield."

"And I should not have had my lovely heart," said the Tin Woodman. "I might have stood and rusted in the forest till the end of the world."

"And I should have lived a coward forever," declared the Lion, "and no beast in all the forest would have had a good word to say to me."

"This is all true," said Dorothy, "and I am glad I was of use to these good friends. But now that each of them has had what he most desired, and each is happy in having a kingdom to rule beside, I think I should like to go back to Kansas."

"The Silver Shoes," said the Good Witch, "have wonderful powers. And one of the most curious things about them is that they can carry you to any place in the world in three steps, and each step will be made in the wink of an eye. All you have to do is to knock the heels together three times and command the shoes to carry you wherever you wish to go."

"If that is so," said the child, joyfully, "I will ask them to carry me back to Kansas at once."

She threw her arms around the Lion's neck and kissed him, patting his big head tenderly. Then she kissed the Tin Woodman, who was weeping in a way most dangerous to his joints. But she hugged the soft, stuffed body of the Scarecrow in her arms instead of kissing his painted face, and found she was crying herself at this sorrowful parting from her loving comrades.

Glinda the Good stepped down from her ruby throne to give the little girl a good-bye kiss, and Dorothy thanked her for all the kindness she had shown to her friends and herself.

Dorothy now took Toto up solemnly in her arms, and having said one last good-bye she clapped the heels of her shoes together three times, saying,

"Take me home to Aunt Em!"

Instantly she was whirling through the air, so swiftly that all she could see or feel was the wind whistling past her ears.

The Silver Shoes took but three steps, and then she stopped so suddenly that she rolled over upon the grass several times before she knew where she was.

At length, however, she sat up and looked about her.

"Good gracious!" she cried.

For she was sitting on the broad Kansas prairie, and just before her was the new farm-house Uncle Henry built after the cyclone had carried away the old one. Uncle Henry was milking the cows in the barnyard, and Toto had jumped out of her arms and was running toward the barn, barking joyously.

Dorothy stood up and found she was in her stocking-feet. For the Silver Shoes had fallen off in her flight through the air, and were lost forever in the desert.

CHAPTER XXIV

HOME AGAIN

AUNT EM had just come out of the house to water the cabbages when she looked up and saw Dorothy running toward her.

"My darling child!" she cried, folding the little girl in her arms and covering her face with kisses; "where in the world did you come from?"

"From the Land of Oz," said Dorothy, gravely. "And here is Toto, too. And oh, Aunt Em! I'm so glad to be at home again!"

L. Frank Baum entertains a group of children with tales of the Land of Oz. Taken at the Hotel del Coronado in 1906.

FATHER GOOSE

1899–1900
by
Angelica Shirley Carpenter
and Jean Shirley

Frank typed his poems himself. He was a fast typist though he used only two fingers. Denslow visited frequently to consult about illustrations. Frank's son Harry wrote later:

I recall that "Den" as we called him, had a striking red vest of which he was inordinately fond. And whenever he came to our house, he would always complain of the heat as an excuse to take off his coat and spend the evening displaying his beautiful red vest. The family used to joke about it among ourselves, but it was a touchy subject with Denslow and we were careful not to say anything about this vanity during his visits.

The book of poems was hard to sell because of a radical idea: Frank and Denslow wanted color on each page. In those days illustrations were usually black and white. Color printing raised the price of a book, and lowered the publisher's profits.

Finally Frank and Denslow found a publisher, George M. Hill. Author and artist shared the cost of production with the Hill Company.

Father Goose, His Book appeared in September 1899, just in time for the Christmas trade. Critics loved the book, but some reviewers thought Denslow's pictures outshone Frank's verses. One critic said it was "almost ablaze with color when compared to the usual children's book of the day."

Father Goose sold 75,000 copies the first year, making it the best-selling children's book of 1899. Frank and Denslow split royalties (payment for each book sold).

Christmas 1899, and all Christmases were happy for the Baums. Son Harry said later:

WE ALWAYS had a Christmas tree, and this was purchased by Father and set up in the front parlor behind drapes that shut off the room. This, Father explained, was done to help Santa Claus, who was a very busy man, and had a good many houses with children to call upon.

Santa Claus (Father) came a little later to deck the tree, and we children heard him talking to us behind the curtains. We tried to peek through cracks in the curtains, but although we could hear Santa

Claus talking, we never managed to see him, and only heard his voice.

On Christmas Day, when the curtains were opened, there was the Christmas tree that Santa Claus had decorated—a blaze of different colors, and the presents for each of the boys stacked below it!

"One Christmas," Harry said, "we had *four* Christmas trees—one for each of the four boys—in the four corners of the room!"

When summer came, the Baums rented a cottage at a Michigan resort town, Macatawa Park. Frank named the cottage The Hyperudenbuttscoff. He painted the name on a sign and hung it outside.

Passersby stopped often, trying to pronounce the strange word and wondering what it meant. Frank got the name from a Chicago museum exhibit. The word referred to a whale's skeleton, but the Baums used it to mean anything hard to describe.

Macatawa Park was on a channel connecting Lake Michigan to the 6-mile-long (9.6-km-long) Lake Macatawa. Frank, who still edited *The Show Window*, commuted to Chicago by boat. He went home to Macatawa on weekends. The Saturday 2:00 P.M. boat from Chicago got him home in time for supper at 7:30.

The Baums found new friends in Michigan. Maud started card clubs, and Frank organized a water carnival, decorating boats and buildings with Japanese lanterns. There were sailing races and dances at the Yacht Club, where Frank started an amateur night, or talent show. Many evenings ended at the Baums', with Frank cooking for the crowd.

Frank smoked cigars, though he knew they were bad for his health. Often he held an unlit cigar in his mouth. One friend said he chewed up about six cigars a day.

When someone asked why he did not light his cigar, Frank insisted that he did, but only when he went swimming. " 'You see,' he explained gravely, 'I can't swim, so when the cigar goes out I know I'm getting over my depth.' "

Frank wrote a book about Macatawa, which he called *Tamawaca Folks, A Summer Comedy.* It was published privately and sold in Macatawa stores. The author's name was given as John Estes Cooke, but Frank's neighbors knew who wrote it.

After *Father Goose* was published, the Baums moved to a new home in Chicago at 68 Humboldt Park Boulevard. At Macatawa, Frank bought a larger cottage.

He named the new cottage The Sign of the Goose, honoring the book that had paid for it. Frank suffered at this time from an attack of facial paralysis. Maud explained later:

His doctor told him to stop writing and do some manual work, so he made a whole set of furniture for our living room—rocker, arm and straight chairs, table, stools and couch—all had leather seats put on with brass strips. Also had a stained glass window with a goose on it . . . On the front porch was a rocking chair, the two sides of which were big geese.

The boys were growing up. Frank Jr., who wanted a military career, applied for admission to Annapolis and West Point. Robert, known as Rob, experimented with electricity. Frank wrote to his brother Harry, now a doctor, "Rob fills the house with electric batteries . . . and we are prepared to hear a bell ring whenever we open a door or step on a stair."

At the dinner table, Maud always tucked her legs under her chair so the boys could not accidentally kick her during debates. Harry said, "To settle the frequent points of dispute which arose, a small shelf was built in the dining room where a dictionary, a single-volumed encyclopedia, and an atlas were kept for quick, convenient reference and decision."

Frank still loved puns, such as this one from *Father Goose:*

> Now once I owned a funny man,
>   A clockwork was inside him;
> You'd be surprised how fast he ran
>   When I was there beside him.
> He was the pride of all the boys
>   Who lived within our town;
> But when this man ran up a hill
>   He always would run down.

Harry said, "When Father made an especially far-fetched pun, we would all laugh uproariously and then reach out our hands to him for any loose change as a reward for laughing."

Soon Frank and Denslow began work on their second

major book. At first they called it *The Emerald City*, until they learned of a publishing superstition: any book with a jewel in the title is bound to fail. So they changed the name to *The Wonderful Wizard of Oz*. For this book, they again insisted on colored illustrations.

George M. Hill refused to publish it, as did every other publisher in Chicago, claiming color was too expensive. The publishers objected to the subject matter as well. In those days, books for children were supposed to be educational and uplifting. This was just a fairy tale—plenty of those old-fashioned stories were already in print.

Finally Hill took a chance, publishing the book in the fall of 1900. It sold for $1.50.

The Wonderful Wizard of Oz contained more than 100 illustrations with 24 color plates. The color of the pictures matched Oz geography, with blue illustrations for the chapters set in the Munchkin Country, green for the Emerald City, and so on.

In the book's introduction, Frank said:

The time has come for a series of newer "wonder tales" in which the stereotyped genie, dwarf and fairy are eliminated, together with all the horrible and blood-curdling incident devised by their authors to point a fearsome moral to each tale.

. . . "The Wonderful Wizard of Oz" was written solely to pleasure children of to-day. It aspires to being a modernized fairy tale, in which the wonderment and joy are retained and the heart-aches and nightmares are left out.

In fact, Frank's story built on the tradition of fantasy adventures. A cyclone carries Dorothy and her dog, Toto, from her Aunt Em and Uncle Henry to the land of the Munchkins, in the fairyland of Oz. Oz, she learns, is surrounded by an uncrossable desert, but Dorothy struggles bravely to get back to Kansas.

At the start of her quest, Dorothy receives silver shoes and a magic kiss from the good Witch of the North. Then she walks across Oz on the yellow brick road. Frank improved on the tradition of the kind friend who helps the heroine. He created the Scarecrow, the Tin Woodman, and the Cowardly Lion. But when Dorothy gets to the Emerald City, she faces the Wizard all alone.

The Wizard will help her, he says, if she kills the Wicked Witch of the West. Frank may have deplored "horrible and blood-curdling incidents," but he knew a scary plot and wicked villains kept readers interested.

By the time Dorothy gets back to Kansas, she has learned that things are not always as they appear to be, and that she has the power within herself to achieve her goals.

Artist Denslow portrayed Dorothy as a chunky farm girl about seven years old, with long brown hair in thick braids.

Frank, the writer, made her practical. She melts the Witch with a pail of water:

The Witch fell down in a brown, melted, shapeless mass and began to spread over the clean boards of the kitchen floor. Seeing that she had really melted away to nothing, Dorothy drew another bucket of water and threw it over the mess. She then swept it all out the door.

Critics liked the book. The *New York Times* wrote: "It will indeed be strange if there be a normal child who will not enjoy the story." Many reviewers compared *The Wizard* to *Alice's Adventures in Wonderland,* the classic fantasy by Lewis Carroll. For a second time, some critics judged Denslow's art to be a greater achievement than Frank's writing. *The Wonderful Wizard of Oz* became the best-selling children's book of 1900.

At first Frank did not realize how well the book was doing. When Maud needed Christmas money, she told Frank to ask his publisher for an advance. This meant payment for books that would be sold later. Frank preferred to wait for his regular payment, but he hated to disappoint the boys. Finally he agreed to ask for $100.

He called on George Hill at the publisher's office. When Hill heard what Frank wanted, he summoned his book-keeper. Hill told the man to write out a check for all the money the firm owed Frank. Frank pocketed the check without looking at it.

When he got home, Maud was ironing his other shirt. Frank gave her the check—made out for $3,432.64! Maud was so excited that she burned a hole in his shirt.

RECOMMENDED READING

Abbott, Donald. *How the Wizard Came to Oz*. New York: Books of Wonder, 1997.

Baum, L. Frank, et al. *The Wonderful Wizard of Oz: The Books of Wonder Edition*. New York: HarperCollins*Publishers* and Books of Wonder, 1987.

Carpenter, Angelica Shirley and Jean Shirley. *L. Frank Baum: Royal Historian of Oz*. Minnesota: Lerner Publications Company, 1992.

Fricke, John. *100 Years of Oz: A Century of Classic Images From The Wizard of Oz Collection of Willard Carroll*. New York: Stewart, Tabori & Chang, 1999.

Fricke, John, Jay Scarfone, and William Stillman. *The Wizard of Oz: The Official 50th Anniversary Pictorial History*. New York: Warner Books, 1989.

Green, Joey. *The Zen of Oz: Ten Spiritual Lessons From Over the Rainbow*. Renaissance Books, 1989.

Hearns, Michael Patrick. *The Annotated Wizard of Oz: A Centennial Edition*. New York: W.W. Norton & Company, 2000.

Riley, Michael O. *Oz and Beyond: The Fantasy World of L. Frank Baum*. The University Press of Kansas, 1997.

Stout, William. *William Stout's World of Oz*. Portfolio of illustrated prints. California: Fine Art Publishing, 1999. (www.fineartpublishing.com)

OZ WEBSITES

www.oz-central.com

Website for the official licensor of the L. Frank Baum Family Trust, and the official distributor of Oz 100th Anniversary Celebration Products.

http://thewizardofoz.warnerbros.com

Official website for the classic 1939 film. Download the movie trailer, shop at the Oz Boutique, check out the photo galleries, even visit Munchkinland and print out coloring book pages.

www.ozclub.org

The International Wizard of Oz Club. Post messages, find out about upcoming conventions and merchandise, check out the latest issue of the club's newsletter, *The Baum Bugle.*

www.eskimo.com/~tiktok

The Wonderful Wizard of Oz website. Maintained by Eric Gjovaag, it contains Frequently Asked Questions about Oz, links to other sites, Oz news, upcoming events, "The Meaning Behind *The Wizard of Oz*," the Tik-Tok Mailing List, and *Wizard of Oz* Lesson Ideas for Teachers.

www.homestead.com/scarecrow/baum~ns.4.html

Benton's Royal Website of Oz. This site gives a brief biography of Baum, and offers links to related sites like *The Land of Oz, The Royal Historians,* and *Oz Films.*